DELIRIUM TREMENS

A Novel Of Destiny

DELIRIUM TREMENS

BY ROBERT REILLY

Mirador Publishing
http://www.miradorpublishing.co.uk

First Published in Great Britain 2011 by Mirador Publishing

First edition: 2011

Any reference to real names and places are purely fictional and are constructs of the author. Any offence the references produce is unintentional and in no way reflect the reality of any locations or people involved.

A copy of this work is available though the British Library.

ISBN : 978-1-908200-15-0

Mirador Publishing
Mirador
Wearne Lane
Langport
Somerset
TA10 9HB

A man, known to those few acquaintances as Kurt Schiff, made his way slowly through the winding streets of Krakow's old town district. The relentless December chill kissed him deeply with every laboured breath as he pulled his collar tight to his neck and advanced into the night. Turning down the cobbled street of ulica Stradomska toward home, he mused at a brief and unexpected sting of nostalgia as memories of his childhood danced momentarily across his mind. The scent of rose petal and orange peel from his mother's garden, a scabbed knee he had received when he'd tumbled from his bicycle, summer evening sunsets whose warmth held the promise of futures unknown. But that was a forgotten time in a forgotten land. And today was the day he would die.

'Hey mister, gimme a fuckin smoke.'

Shaken from his reverie, he became aware of three drunken girls directly in his path.

'Are you fuckin deaf or something, old man? Do you have a smoke or what?'

Kurt flinched at the Polish gutter slang favoured by the city's youth. Ambivalence and lethargy regarding their own lives and society manifested in speech, a vocal affront to tradition and structure. He eyed them in disgust, barely in their teens, painted whores. Short skirts revealing stick legs, bloodshot eyes revealing nothing but emptiness and hate.

'Sorry, I don't smoke,' he replied.

'My friend will suck your cock for a hundred złoty.'

A chorus of cackled laughter followed this as Kurt pushed by and hurried on his way.

'Probably too old to get it up.'

Left with this parting sentiment, he continued toward the old Jewish district of Kazimierz where he resided. The encounter had darkened his spirits somewhat. Krakow, he reflected, a bitch betrayed. The stench of urine and the rotting flesh of the city's open wounds made him gag, like a rat crawling down his throat. Her adulterer suckling at the teat of the whore, laying with the nigger and the Turk. It's no wonder she weeps such poison tears.

After some time, he arrived at the place he had reluctantly called home for many years. The cold plays havoc with the locks on these old buildings, joints swelled and dry, aching with bone deep chill. It takes a minute for the key to find purchase and the effort draws a wince across Kurt's face. It seems at this fine age that the minutiae of everyday life take more effort than it's worth. Tying a shoelace, dragging a steel razor across the pock-marked landscape of your jaw, taking a breath…. No time left now. I can feel there's not long before a stranger comes knocking and I want to be prepared. With grim resolve, he made his way up the ramshackle staircase of the old apartment block, each step shooting a jolt of pain through his core. At the forth floor he pauses momentarily as a wave of dizziness threatens to send him back down the stairwell. The shadow of a wry smile touches his face and then melts to disgust. To be trapped in this bag of brittle bones and dust. To be victimised by putrid organs burping out their last. To feel the sting as you piss and the cramps as you void your bowels. What a piece of work is a man, how noble in reason, how infinite in faculty, in form and moving how express and admirable, in action how like an angel, in apprehension how like a god!

The memory of the great bard's words uttered by that Danish prince mocked Kurt's wizened state. But by God he was great once. Noble and strong when a nation needed to be guided by reason and not by the fickle flame of emotional fervour. Their vision had been unique and boundless, it's execution a masterpiece of function. No time to reminisce; time is of the essence.

The man known as Kurt Schiff hastened into his apartment, dropped his keys on the hall table and removed his overcoat. He stamped the excess snow off his black painted leather shoes and placed them neatly by the door before slipping into his house shoes. Otherwise he liked to be sharply dressed, even indoors. He wore a well cut charcoal grey three-piece suit, a powder blue dress shirt and a burgundy tie knotted with a double Windsor. Acquaintances and neighbours would comment favourably on how nice it was to see a man of his years take care with how he presented himself. The old ladies behind the counter in the local butchers and *piekarnicze* would coo and wink and say what a stylish man he was. There's few gentlemen like him left in the world, they would say. They had no idea how right they were.

In the dark enclave of his living room, Kurt laid his suit jacket neatly across the back of a rickety wooden stool and switched on a small table lamp. He exhaled deeply as he took in his surroundings. The moth-eaten couch. The stained wood table where he took his solitary meals. The nicotine wallpaper that had begun to curl and bubble. The small television set whose message heralded the end of civilisation with manic white smiles as they tap danced into the abyss. Lowering himself onto the couch, he reached for a bottle on the coffee table and poured himself a generous brandy. There was such satisfying promise in the delicate tinkle as the glass filled and the rustic apple aroma as it assailed the senses. Kurt drank deeply, feeling the burn spread through his body and quiet his mind. Loosening his tie and rolling up his shirt sleeves, his glance fell to his upper left forearm. Taking the forefinger of his right hand, he tentatively traced the sequence of numbers crudely tattooed on his flesh. Faded and blurred by time and mottled skin, it was still a mark that provoked in all a deep resonance to the core of their being. A mark that demanded a reappraisal of one's own humanity, that you stare into yourself and wonder at the mask that stares back at

3

you. How long can you stare into the eyes behind that mask before you feel a blood churning scream rise from your stomach and devour you?

I remember it well, clearer than I have done in years. In the beginning they had just used indelible ink to mark the clothes of those infirmed or ripe for execution, however, the stripping of corpses and the increasing pile of bodies made this system impractical when attempting to identify remains. And so in 1941, on an icy autumn morn in Auschwitz, a keen and ambitious soul implemented a new permanent method of identification. In its infancy, the procedure involved a specially designed metal stamp, where interchangeable numbers comprised of needle arrays would be driven into the prisoner's chest. Ink was then used on the bloody fissures for lasting effect. Trial and error streamlined the process to a single needle device, which traced a serial number on the forearm into which the ink could seep. This keen and ambitious soul received much praise and adulation for such initiative and creativity and was duly promoted to Standartenführer within the hallowed ranks of the SS. Known then as Wilhelm Jodl, this proud young officer stood tall, his almost delicate features accentuated by a sharp jaw and piercing grey eyes. Known now as Kurt Schiff, the irony does not escape him that the very same ink would provide the sheep's clothing for the wolf when the horns of the great hunt sounded.

The bells of St. Catherine's church echoed through the night, drawing Kurt from his trance as he moved to the window to take in the darkness beyond. A light snow drifted on the wind, blanketing the small streets in silence. He shifted his focus to his own reflection in the glass and considered the creature that stood before him. The fine silver hair drawn across his pale skull. The birdlike nose atop the thin lips that sneered back at him. The piercing grey eyes, although muddied with ochre, were the only recognisable reminder of Standartenführer Jodl. As a young officer, he had been chosen especially to be stationed at Auschwitz due to his prowess in the medical field. His research in criminal biology had contributed significantly to the racial profiling of the asocials and their subsequent internment in the prison camps. His research was particularly applicable to the gypsies, whose sloping foreheads, large eye sockets and strong jaw bones were consistent with the physical identification markers of the born criminal. Further research showed the *ziguener* to be genetically disposed to laziness and vagrancy. This, combined with the tainted blood of centuries of slumming in the miscreant cess pool, had exposed the need to deal with the gypsy plague on a grander scale.

How surprisingly vital their breed turned out to be, mused Kurt. They lasted so much longer then the other test subjects and their physical endurance was exemplary. His mind was cast back to one particular gypsy bitch, whom while in camp had given birth to twins, one male one female. It took three officers to drag her screaming and cursing into laboratory five, all the time pleading for her babies. During the sterilization tests, as the x-rays seared through her loins, she still called for her young long after others had perished. When a syringe rich with a chemical cocktail succeeded in fusing her uterus shut, she remained conscious, wailing for mercy for her little ones. The attending physician Dr. Clauberg, who had a penchant for experimenting on twins, had suggested that this woman's physical stamina may have passed to her young. He had long been curious as to whether two twins when surgically sewn together would experience a fusing of flesh and bone akin to that of conjoined infants. The horror in the mother's eyes remained fixed long after her heart had surrendered on seeing the first scalpel flourish find it's mark.

A slight movement of shadow beyond his reflection drew his eye to a human form framed in the doorway of his living room. A sharp, icy current passed through him as he turned to face his guest.

'How long have you been standing there?' he spat.

A heavy silence filled the room.

'I knew you'd be coming, you know.'

Kurt expected this revelation to unnerve his guest, but the stranger just continued to hold his gaze and advanced slowly into the room. Kurt, who prided himself on being a sharp judge of a man, was growing more uneasy as the seconds drew out. He was, in his prime, a master of psychological warfare and he thrived on confrontations such as this. The subtle power dynamics of any altercation could be manipulated through word and gesture to bring the hardest adversary whimpering to his knees. Why was it that now, when the stakes were highest, that he knew in his heart that this was a game he had already lost?

With a heavy sigh, Kurt lazily gestured to an armchair and lowered himself back into the couch. He tossed down the remains of his brandy in one and with glassy eyes considered his guest.

'Would you begrudge a condemned man a last smoke?'

The stranger took a seat in the armchair opposite and resumed his steady gaze. Kurt eyed him with curiosity. It was difficult to figure the man's age. The shadows played across his face, giving the unsettling illusion of both youthfulness and the haggard features of a life long lived. The closely cropped hair and the thick stubble of his jaw was a deep red with traces of amber and darker tones. His slim build was wrapped tightly in a heavy overcoat and his hands were buried deep in the pockets. His eyes captivated Kurt. The gaze was slightly unfocused and the pale green of his irises swam imperceptibly giving the impression of a man mired in the fog of a waking dream.

'I'll take that as a no then, will I?' sneered the old man and reached for a battered pack of Mocne from the coffee table. He cursed himself as a trembling hand lit the cigarette on the third attempt and a hacking cough shuddered through his frame with the first drag.

'Still worth it,' he grimaced when the spasms had subsided.

'You know, my friend, if you think I'm going to give you the satisfaction of seeing me beg for this pitiful excuse for a life, you're sorely mistaken. Is that what you want? Do you want me to fall to my fucking knees and say how sorry I am for these things I did? How, if I could, I'd change everything and atone for my sins? Well fuck you!' hissed Kurt, spittle flying from his lips.

'You think you can sit there and judge me, condemn me. You have no idea what it takes, no idea what sacrifices have to be made to ensure a better world for the future of humanity. I've watched and listened while you weak-minded puppets hide behind the liberal rhetoric of your corrupt fathers, while you open the flood gates and let in the waves of human filth from the east. Wasting time and money treating the symptoms of this pestilence, instead of taking a blade and cutting out the tumour. There isn't a hand bold enough or steady enough in these great lands to make that cut and, for that, I am truly sorry.'

Kurt took a moment to regain his composure, slightly breathless from the exertion. He smoothed back his thin hair with a moist palm and, leaning forward, crushed the butt of his cigarette into a heavy glass ashtray.

'Fine,' he muttered, as the fight drained from him. 'Do what you came here to do.' 'After all,' he added with a wry smile, 'You're only following orders.'

The stranger rose from the armchair and soundlessly moved to where Kurt now stood. Face to face, Kurt was transfixed by the deep sadness in the man's eyes. He leaned in slowly, almost tenderly, so that his lips were close to the old man's ear. The soft whisper was the last thing Kurt heard before his lifeless body crumpled to the ground.

'So she's riding me hard cowgirl style and screaming like a fucking banshee, and all I can think about is this great big fucking dog that's eyeballing me from the corner of the room.'

Despite myself I smile, as the kid relates yet another account of some recent sexual misadventure. He's not a bad kid after all. Not even a kid. He's got to be in his late twenties, but has the twitchy, nervous demeanour and the skinny frame of an adolescent. I pick at the label on my beer bottle, third of the day, and take a deep swig, grateful as I feel the shadows of last night slowly ebb away. The gloom is replaced by an uneasy giddiness, but I'm old hat at this dance so I gesture to the bartender to whisky me.

'Bear, she calls it, and it's such a huge fucking beast that when she walks it she uses a great big bloody harness thing. Anyway, it's giving me the stink eye from the corner and I'm thinking, Jesus, what if the dog thinks I'm attacking this woman, what with her screaming like I'm gutting her with a hunting knife.'

Pedro sets up a shot glass in front of me and pulls a bottle of Old Duke from the shelf. Normally I wouldn't touch this shit, but it's actually the best you can get in these parts. If I was to drink the local Guatemalan fare, I'm likely to be half blind and bleeding from my rectum by the third glass. The first goes down like a dream, calming the nerves. The burn in my pipes cools to a dull throb, and the beer chaser puts out the flash fires in my ostrich. I pat down my shirt pockets in search of a smoke to put the icing on the cake, and luck upon a pack of Payasos from the night before.

'So there I am, bucking like a mule,' continues Johnny Boy in his cheeky cockney chatter, relishing the small crowd of afternoon drinkers lined at the bar listening to this epic tale. Mostly old timers hanging on his every word, both nourished and saddened by the eroticism, as ghosts in a young man's world. 'And suddenly the dog is on his feet and clambering up onto the end of the bed. She's grinding hard and doesn't notice a fucking thing. The dog goes straight for my balls and starts licking like there's no tomorrow. She notices I'm paralysed with fear, sees what the dog's at, and tells me to relax and enjoy it. Like it happens all the fucking time!'

'Jesus Christ, that's messed up,' chimes in Gerd the Head, a retired merchant sailor from Holland. 'Isn't that like bestiality or something? I'm sure you ran for the hills.'

'What are you kidding me? Best threesome I ever had, my friend.'

Laughter fills the bar in disbelief and appreciation of this new addition to the seemingly limitless depravity of Johnny Boy's sexual conquests. I motion to Pedro to stick another whisky in, since the first went down so well. With the edge well and truly off, I throw an eye around the rest of the bar. I swear to God, most of these people never leave this place, cowering in here like refugees from the war of the living, a refuge for sinners. Everybody's got a story in here, most of the time recounted as if from another life, another body, another soul. For many, this place has been chosen as the last port in the storm, but for many others, they're just lost. There is one thing in common for us all though, and that is that time is measured by the glass, and on it ticks.

Even in the shade, it's still too warm for my liking. The shafts of sunlight beat down through the open windows, the light thick with the dust of the outside streets. This slick, clammy heat is not conducive to a chipper state of mind, so I mostly spend the afternoons in here reading books. This town is peppered with second-hand book stores, filled with the detritus from travellers passing through. Literary fiction, biographies, short stories, pulp, chick lit, fantasies, whodunits, whydunits, whatever's going. My tastes vary depending on the mood and variety, I'm told, is the spice of life.

'What's the good word, Jakey?'

I turn to see Lucas sidle up beside me at the bar and clap me jovially on the back. I flinch momentarily at this affectionate bastardisation of my name, but in truth, I'm pleased to see him. He is one of my only confidants in these dark days, and the closest thing I've been able to call a friend in a long time.

'When did you get back from Europe? Colder than a witch's tit this time of year, I imagine. Any problems?'

'Not that I recall anyway,' I reply half-heartedly.

I drain my bottle of beer to quell the unease that bubbles up inside my chest. Sleepless nights, waking dreams, blackouts and the permanent haze of shifting realities that my appetites afford me have left my mind sick and my memory broken. The harder I try to grasp at the filament of truth, the harder it becomes to distinguish the real from the imagined.

'This man looks like he could use a drink,' suggests Lucas, accurately at that. 'Give me two shots of that Zacapa you keep up there, chief, and beer chasers.'

Pedro racks up two tumblers and portions out a healthy dram of rum in each. Dark and oaky with plays of crimson light dancing through it, this was for sure the antidote to my woes.

'Salud!' comes the call, and the juice is dropped.

Spirit emboldened, I consider my friend as he exchanges pleasantries with the bartender. A curious character to say the least. A few years my senior, somewhere in his forties, he sports stylish black framed glasses with pink tinted lenses, and always wears a black shirt of silk or chiffon or some other expensive fabric. Combined with a gift for eloquent speech and a refined manner, this was almost absurdly counterbalanced with a distinctly masculine physicality. His gait and movements suggest a labouring background, and his neck and forearms are roped with lean muscle. A thick, knotted scar runs from the top of his left cheekbone to his temple, all the more prominent due to the blackness of his hair. Since making his acquaintance, I think I've heard at least eight different versions of how this scar came to be, ranging from sporting injuries, car crashes, heroic interventions and brain surgery. I fear that some truths can break a man, and so I happily entertain these fictions.

'What have you been up to Lucas? How's business treating you?' I enquire.

Lucas makes his money applying his gift for languages to interpreting the legalese of business contracts between large firms. In cases where contracts are drawn up in a language foreign to his employers, he would be charged with translating the document and deciphering the subtleties of the script. His skill lay in his understanding of cultural difference, using the interpretative nature of language to expose weaknesses in the agreement, affording his employers a stronger bargaining position. A slick-lipped advisor, whispering sweet nothings into the grey king's ear. Although Lucas does not like to talk money, balking at the subject as if tawdry, I imagine his services do not come cheap.

'Oh, you know how it is. Man's gotta make a living,' he smirks, affecting a mock Texan drawl. 'By the by, I happened to spy your little lolita in all her beauty and splendour down by the market stalls. Would it be presumptuous of me to assume you'll be paying your lady a visit tonight? Engage in a spot of coitus perhaps? One must indulge in earthly pleasures while the fruit is ripe for plucking, my friend. After all, as Mark Twain put it,' he adds, tipping me a wink, 'Of the delights of this world man cares most for sexual intercourse, yet he has left it out of his heaven.'

The mention of Sofia awakes sweet, lustful memories in me. My hand lightly tracing the contours of her nubile flesh. The youthful eagerness of her tongue in my mouth. The dark heat of her wet sex pulling me into her, owning me. Shit, the last time I managed to get some proper winks was in her bed, spent bodies entwined, the warm flutter of her breath on my skin, the funk of our fucking thick in the air.

'You know, it has been a while. I think I'll give her a bell and take her for a night on the tiles. You got any plans for the evening?'

'I am nothing if not a creature of the night, Jacob. I'll be around.'

I gesture to Pedro that I'm off, and exchange the customary nods and grunts with the stool monkeys who cling to the bar for dear life. Drinks are put on the tab, whatever that entails. My relationship to this den of iniquity and its proprietor is ill-defined. My mind struggles to capture when it was I first walked through the door of Kelly's in search of my brother Caleb, but the moment, and the time since, have become blurred and crippled. Yet again unease threatens to sink me, so I push it down in my gut. Months? A year? Two years? The only thing I'm certain of is that I'm locked in a deadly embrace, and this grim waltz is taking me deep into the darkness.

Outside, the blinding light of the mid-afternoon shoots painful darts through my retinas. A thin layer of sweat immediately coats my skin and the heat rising from the cobble streets is tangible. I'm not made for this weather. I'm not made for any weather come to think of it. The grey showers that washed out the Dublin streets of my childhood have ill prepared me for such things. I squint down towards the town square, the backdrop of Volcán de Agua quivering in the distant haze.

The pastel shades of Antigua's quiet streets are blanched with sunlight and those with any sense have retreated into the cool shade. The bells of La Merced draw my gaze up the street, a towering ornate structure of faith. What the hell, a few minutes out of this stew will help me get my head together for the walk home. The kick of the drink and the heat of the streets make for unwelcome bedfellows, so I duck in through the heavy oak doors for a spell.

The cold of the granite shadows is an instant and welcome pleasure. I've always enjoyed the inside of a church, even long after the love that first brought me there faded and died. The artistry of the sculpture and the grandeur of the space, combined with the heady aroma of incense and candle wax, always struck a deep chord. Every footfall and hushed prayer swallowed up by the echoing silence of the chamber. The awe that struck me was not God's love, but the toil and labour of man in pursuit of such a thing.

Only a few congregants littered the pews, old Mayan women in traditional dress, lips moving silently as they finger their beads. Despite the sparse flock, a priest was sermonising from the pulpit. My lingo español skills are rudimentary, but as his sermon runs I manage to grasp a snatch of scripture that echoes from my youth.

'...*In the beginning was the Word, and the Word was with God, and the Word was God. He was in the beginning with God.*'

The priest's pitted jowls sit heavy on the white collar that marks his faith. He wears his beliefs for all to see, his relationship to the divine on display for those who would judge or revere him. On his face he wears his demons. The broken blood vessels snake across his sallow cheeks, cracks through which a scream can be glimpsed beneath the flesh.

'...*All things were made through Him, and without Him nothing was made that was made.*'

Maybe knowledge of the dark is required for a true understanding. How strange for a man to wear all he is. What do I wear? It would seem to me I wear nothing, but perhaps that's my heaviest robe. My head starts to feel agitated and a churning in my gut says it's time I beat an exit. My feet don't make a sound as I move for the door, so much so that I wonder if I'm here at all. The disembodiment that accompanies this thought compounds the waves of nausea rising inside of me. As I leave I turn once more to take in the scene.

'...*In Him was life, and the life was the light of men. And the light shines in the darkness, and the darkness did not comprehend it.*'

A jolt runs through my body like the pulse of a muscle just before sleep comes. The priest's eyes locked with mine. He sees me. He knows me.

Gotta pick up Finn from the old bat upstairs who fucking eyes me like I'm Joe fucking homeless who just shat himself and my heart is thumping hard in my chest and she's asking me if I've heard of such and such neighbour's daughter getting up the duff and there's lipstick on her yellow teeth and she suspected the little whore was no good and the sweat is running down my ribcage and she's watered my plants and mister old bat 's screaming for his dinner and all I want to do is get in to my fucking flat away from the noise and her eyes.

I grab Finn in my arms mumbling apologies and thanks and apologies in pig Spanish as I hurry downstairs and let myself in to the flat. I deposit Finn in his basket and grab a half full bottle of vodka from the sideboard and drink deep from the neck. The tremor in my hands causes the lip of the bottle to rattle off my teeth as I drink. A death rattle. The writhing spasm of a fool trying to squirm out of the grip of the reaper. There's no question that the sickness is getting worse. It used to be that the horrors would come only in the mornings, dispatched soon there after with the tall blood of the virgin. Celery optional. Of late, the jarring nerve scream is always only a heartbeat away, its sick breath on my neck.

The spirit hits my guts with a white hot burn, and I barely get my drawers down and my ass to the pot before the putrid scutter explodes from my bowels. I dry heave as a horrifying odour of vomit and sweaty cheese fills my nostrils, but the disgust is short lived, replaced by the euphoric calm of release. This is a committed relationship after all, and one must take the bad with the good. It's better than being alone.

I flop down on the couch, a physical, mental and emotional carcass. Finn jumps up and slobbers all over my face, his tail tapping a jaunty tune on my side.

'Hey guy. What's the story? Hope that cantankerous old slag upstairs has been feeding you well. Let me have a look at you,' I say as I lift him. Since I've never been what you would call an animal person, it continuously surprises me at how I've taken to the little runt. A ways back, I was on my stagger home, cutting down an alleyway where some street kids were fucking about, smashing glasses and huffing paint thinner and such. I would have passed on my way, but a weak yelp drew my attention to the focus of their sport, these black eyed ghouls, their minds itching from the glue bags. This shaking wretch of a pup, patchy hair matted with shit, was cornered between a discarded refrigerator and a pile of wood pallets, while eager boots rained down bruises on his bony frame. My shouts sent the rats scarpering into the shadows and even though he was half dead, he still had the pluck to snarl and snap at me when I took him in my arms. There are animals that take a licking and role over and die, and there are animals that are born to scrape and claw their way through the hardships of this thing called life. Even after I cleaned him up good and filled his belly, he's still one of the ugliest sonsabitches going. In my more maudlin stupors I concede that this adds to his charm, and since then we've kept good company, Finn and me.

After some rest, my mood begins to pick up. By now I've grown accustomed to this carnival of peaks and troughs.

'I think I'll make a night of it buddy. A shower, a shit and a shave, and I'm ready to set the world on fire. What do you say?' Finn shows his support of this motion with a quizzical expression, followed by an enthusiastic exploration of his genitals. 'I thought you'd agree old chap. Now pick me out a clean shirt while I go get this show on the road.' I trot off to the bathroom, eager for the night's pleasures. As with anything worth its salt in life, it's the moment just before you indulge that is the most tantalising. With vice, these sensations are heightened all the more. Nerves tingle, the pulse quickens, the mouth waters, the cock hard and the pussy wet. These moments are pure and guiltless, but man cannot live on amuse-bouche alone, when the banquet of eternity is laid out before him.

Caleb and I were born dizygotic twins, or fraternal twins as it's more commonly known. The physical similarities we shared as young boys were mostly due to being born the same age and having a similar wiry build, as opposed to any chromosomal disposition. Born when our parents were already in the late summer of their lives and had given up hope of conceiving, our birth was heralded by our doting mother as a gift from God. My parents' faith, which had always been an unquestionable foundation of their existence, was further deepened by our unexpected arrival, hence our mother's insistence that we be christened from the good book. Any preconceptions that we were serene waifs, bestowed from on high, came crashing to the ground as soon as we hit the table. We were expelled from the birth canal kicking and screaming at each other, this dynamic defining our relationship as we grew up. As young boys we would listen wide eyed and eager to our mother's embellished tales of this titanic birth battle. Ultrasound images of in-utero gladiators strangling each other with the umbilical chord. Foetal fingers, slimed in afterbirth, gouging at the blind eyes of his adversary.

Although it's the cardinal rule of the parental code that you must never admit to favouring one child over another, it became clear early on that Caleb was the apple of my mother's eye, and I my father's. Caleb had the curly black mop of hair of our father, but in character he was his mother's son. He was an emotional child, his mood shifting manically from giddy highs to fearsome lows, attacking interests with passionate zeal, only to tire shortly after and shift his focus to some new pursuit. He burned with a fierce intelligence, but his inherent rebellious nature made his relationship with school teachers tenuous on the best of days, and on many occasions our parents were called to interventions. I, on the other hand was quiet and bookish like our old man, but with a shock of ginger hair like my mother. I have fond memories of drizzly Sunday afternoons with him, sitting by the kitchen table carefully applying paint to model aeroplanes with tiny brushes, while he'd tell stories in his hushed lilt. Even back then, before the darkness descended on him for good, he wore thick eyeglasses and squinted heavily to apply detail to these works of art. Through the window I could see Caleb, splashing around in the back garden, muddied and drenched, trying to find toads or snails to terrorise. Like our mother, he had a natural artistic and musical flare, for which I had always harboured feelings of sour resentment. I would spend many hours practicing scales on the guitar until my fingers were raw and calloused, memorising classical pieces so that every note was exact. Caleb, however, had a gift for improvising melodies, imbuing musical pieces with stark emotion and life to the joy of his captivated audiences. In our teenage years, his irreverent nonchalance made him popular with the local girls, and the bane of their poor mothers' lives. Me and the other neighbourhood lads were carried along in his wake, troublemakers and rabble rousers led by the one and true king. Thick as thieves, brothers in arms, challenging the world to a brawl.

Differences aside, our bond as brothers was strong and we were naturally drawn to each other, and all through our childhood I can't recall many occasions that we were apart. Long before we could articulate the tensions between our characters, we knew that we were the same yet not the same, the balance of each other. I was nourished and fascinated by Caleb's unquenchable zest for adventure and his brazen affront to the authorities I feared and respected. Alternatively, he found solace from his private madness in the even, comforting embrace of my rationale. I was his touchstone to reality, the centre to which his swinging pendulum came to rest. I loved him wholly, as brothers do, right up to the moment he wrenched my world apart by taking away everything that gave my life meaning. All that I have left to live for now is the moment when that debt is settled, and my brother lies dead by my hand.

I stop in at a tienda on the central square to buy a pack of smokes and a cold can of Gallo, and settle myself on a bench to check out the scene. This is more like it. The sun's gone down and the night air is cool and dry. This is my favourite time of day, and I like to sit and watch the transition. The day traders pack up their wares, cashew boys, balloon men, chiglet chicks. Their clientele are the moon-faced tourists with their white socks and sandals, paying off the debt of their first world liberal guilt on local junk. The night traders are a different breed, oozing onto the streets as the music from the bars and restaurants beats out the pulse. Slick young Latino boys with night club flyers, eyeing their prey as fair haired tourist girls giggle and smile. High-heeled beauties with mocha skin and inviting eyes. Street urchins with quick fingers darting in and out of the shadows. Hooded street chemists slinging herbs and potions to the soul sick. Flesh dealers, vampires, cannibals. The night is a play and everybody has their part. And what a stage this is. The ornate Spanish colonial style facades and arches, lit from below with spectacular effect. The lush greenery of the square's foliage and the scent of blossom and lime. The cacophony of street sounds and the rich smoky aromas from the food stalls; grilled pork, citrus tomato and coriander. On the horizon, the majesty of Volcán de Fuego is set against an azure sky, a constant lava stream bubbling from its mouth. The night is decadent and full of possibility, a living, breathing entity. I drag deep on my smoke and drain my beer. I am a child of the night.

Beyond the locals, the town is beset by an international plague; locusts, leeches, parasites. Gathered under the pretence of anonymity in the verges but in truth in search of self, wishing to be reborn in the stifling claustrophobia. Suffocated into being, choked to life. Nobody is who they say they are but that's alright, lies sit easy in this town and we allow these delicate charades lest the whole system crumbles to our feet and we are revealed. I too am a parasite but I feed off myself, gnawing away at flesh and spirit until I am nothing but a walking death mask. But this relationship between me and I swings both ways and I watch with morbid joy as I devour myself.

'*Mi amor*, it's been too long. I was beginning to think you didn't love me any more,' pouts Sofia with feigned hurt as she pulls me in for a warm embrace. Jesus, she smells great. I nuzzle deep into her thick mane and kiss the nape of her neck, her skin soft and scented with fragrant oils.

'Come in and let me take care of you, my sweet Jacob.' I love the way she says my name, with that beautiful, delicate Latina cadence.

I follow her inside, watching her as she moves. It's like she walks on air, soundless and ethereal. She turns her head and throws me a mischievous smile that stirs my loins. She's wearing a light summer dress that falls to her mid thigh and her hair is loose and tumbling down her slender back. Her long legs are of a soft caramel, and she wears a silver charm bracelet on her left ankle. I drink her in like a man dying of thirst.

Her place is an open plan loft which has a somewhat Moroccan feel to it, with patterned wall hangings and colourful cushions strewn about. It's warm and inviting with the aroma of incense lingering. Her bed is similarly adorned with silken throw pillows, and a thick hand-woven bed spread. She fixes me a drink by the kitchen counter.

'When are you going to be done with this bad business Jacob? You look like shit.' She pronounces this *sheet*. Even her curses are cute. She hands me a tumbler of gold tequila and, fixing me with a look of genuine concern, touches my face softly with her hand.

'My pale Irish. Have they told you for how long this is going to continue? It's just not fair,' she says, suddenly getting upset.

'They can't expect you to keep working for them without giving you what they promised. You're not made for these things. It's obviously killing you.' I put down the glass and take her in my arms.

'I didn't know you cared so much, baby,' I say with attempted frivolity, but unease marks my tone. I had entered into a world I knew nothing about, dizzy and blinded with thoughts of vengeance. Caleb was so close now I could feel him, smell him. I had come too far and sacrificed too much to stop now, even if the cost was my soul. From the moment I agreed to enter this grim covenant, it became clear that a door was opened that could never be closed. There is no place for regret, no place for falter. I've become the animal I seek, and I'll follow this path down into the void.

'Listen,' I say, handing her a glass. 'I'll talk to Pedro about it and see if he can get me a meet with Uri. But tonight I just want to forget about it and spend some quality time with my favourite girl. Deal?'

Her features soften with this reassurance, and a soft smile touches her lips. Fuck. Even the mere mention of that vulpine bastard gets the hair on my arms and nape standing to attention. How does that old wives tale go, it's when someone walks across your grave? In Uri's case he'd probably dig you up and sodomise your corpse while wearing your face as a skin mask. Having a sit down with Uri does not rate high on my list of things I like to do for fun but Sofia is right, I'm turning into a ghost. I can feel the thin threads that hold my mind together start to twist and tear, visible beneath the sick pallor of my skin. I need to shake off this bad buzz so I raise my glass to hers.

'As we say back home, '*Go mbeirimíd beo ar an am seo arís!*'' Sofia wrinkles her nose and gives me a quizzical look.

'May we be alive at the same time next year!' I grin, and down the tequila.

'Asshole,' she says smiling, and tosses hers down in one.

I lie back on the soft bed and listen to Sofia chatter on about her friends and family, about her mother's hip operation and her friend Lucia's new boyfriend. She's talking about the problems with the new government's hard-handed tactics with local officials in the highlands, and how they're kidnapping children to secure votes. She's showing me her latest sculpture and explaining the symbolism of the piece, how it represents the dichotomy of the modern ethos, the constant struggle of the inner self. It kind of looks to me like a vagina with teeth, but I'm more than content to lie here, smiling and nodding. The tequila is hitting me nice and my head swims in appreciation. It's the good stuff too, not that corner-store donkey piss you see the local sots drinking, giving them the ball juice to go home and knock their wives about. I take another drink and then suck on a slice of lemon. The nerves in my jaw come alive with this not altogether unpleasant taste sensation. Sofia's down on her knees by the bed chopping out some fat lines of blanco onto a small mirror. She talks incessantly as she goes about her toil, the razor blade making a fine powder. With one hand she holds back her hair and, taking a rolled up fifty quetzal note, she dusts off a thick line. I can see the explosion behind her black eyes and her top lip trembles ever so slightly. My cock suddenly becomes rock hard. I take the note and snort a line, feeling the chemical honey drop in my throat almost instantly. A shiver of pleasure whips through my veins and my face feels like it's swaddled in cotton. My heart is hammering in my chest, and I can feel the blood rush through every capillary. My head feels like a balloon that has come loose from my body and is floating away. Sofia reaches forward, slowly rubbing my cock through my jeans. She's looking at me with those dark, sultry eyes and, biting her lower lip, massages my cock so that it stiffens and strains against the material.

'You're such a bad boy, Jacob,' she says all innocent like, her cheeks slightly flushed. 'You've made me all wet.'

I can't contain myself any longer. I get to my feet and throw her onto the bed as she giggles with delight. I reach under her summer dress and pull her panties down, lifting her legs up so I can get them all the way off. I push her legs open and start feasting hungrily on her, pushing my tongue into the soft pink flesh. She wasn't lying, she's soaking wet, and she starts to moan with pleasure as she pushes my head further between her legs and pumps her hips rhythmically. I explore every part of her, my face wet with her excitement, every stroke making her swell with arousal. Her breathing becomes short and strained and as she starts to push herself tight against me, I can feel she's about to come hard. She digs her nails into the back of my head, crying out in pleasure as she shudders to a climax. Her hips jerk and spasm as she rides the orgasm all the way to the end. I pull off my shirt and clamber out of my jeans and shorts, my rigid cock swollen and eager. Sofia pulls her dress over her head, revealing her small perfect breasts, her dark brown nipples stiff and erect. She turns onto her hands and knees, sticking her ass high in the air and looking back over her shoulder invitingly. I thrust myself deep inside her and start pumping hard, my hands grabbing her smooth brown buttocks as I feel myself swell with pleasure. Her slippery sex grips me tight, and she works her hips back and forward in rhythm with me. I reach around and work her with my fingers until she comes again, panting and squealing, giddy and breathless. I can feel the head of my cock deep in her, ready to explode. My hands grip her tiny waist and her ass jiggles as I slam into her, again and again. I come so hard I nearly pass out, clenching as I drive it home. We both fall down on the bed, sweaty and spent, our bodies slick from the zeal of passion.

'I needed that. You're the best, baby,' she moans, her hair damp and strewn across her face. These are the things people say, just another part of the ritual, pandering to the fragility of the male ego. But I am a man so I'll take it all the same.

'Yes indeed,' I acquiesce, lighting a smoke and filling our glasses. 'What say you to a night on the town, *chica*? Go get on your dancing shoes and we'll paint it red.'

'Sounds great, *papito*. I told Raul I'd come by El Espejo later and check out his new show. I think you'll enjoy it, get your mind off things, no? Anyway, let's have a few more lines before we go.'

'Jesus, I weep for the youth of today. You're gonna give this old man a heart attack,' I say as I reach for a note and get down to business.

I like this place, despite it being a pretentious, post-modern wank parlour. It's called El Matadero, or slaughterhouse, and favours the titular aesthetic of industrial wrought iron and minimalism. The bar stretches the length of the wall in the massive inner chamber, which leads out into a number of smaller rooms. High tables and stools with hard metallic surfaces dot the main chamber, comfort having being sacrificed at the altar of artistic expression. No bother. I feel more at ease these days in dark cellars, my senses numbed by shadows and the dull base thud. And let's not forget my lady elixir, whose sweet kisses keep the terrors at bay. I go to the bar and order a couple of vodkas, mouthing my request over the noise. The thick beat is accompanied by intermittent animal screams which are having a twitchy effect on my powdered mind, so I take a wander to see where Sofia's got to.

The clientele is an eclectic mix, money men from the capital, local art and culture types, wheelers and dealers, movers and shakers. Moving through the crowd, I catch a glimpse of Lucas at the other side of the room talking to two older men whose appearance suggests middle-eastern origin. For a moment, his gaze scans the crowd and meets mine, but his expression doesn't register anything, returning his attention to his companions. The air is thick, a clot of perfumes, sweat and dry ice. Physical contact is unavoidable as I push across the room, the heat of foreign bodies sending a wave of repulsion through me. I'm too wired for this slow dance. When I emerge from the flesh pool I realise it's not Lucas at all, but a much younger man. He levels me with a peculiar look and I feel the skin on my brain begin to crawl like maggots are nesting in the flesh.

'Do we know each other?' he asks, his eyes heavily lidded behind horn-rimmed glasses and a smile playing on his lips.

The sound is distorted as if I'm underwater and my vision blurs and ripples. My heart is hammering in my chest and panic sits uneasily in my gut waiting to pounce.

'I'm sorry,' I mutter, 'I thought you were someone else.'

Shit, I can't get a grip on this high, and the fear is starting to rise. Just got to ride it out. He takes his hand and lightly touches me on the arm. The sensation of his olive skin makes me want to vomit and run screaming, but his grip is now holding me where I stand.

'No problem,' he whispers, 'it wouldn't be the first time.' I can feel a dribble of cold sweat run down my spine. His sick smile looks like a ghastly meat mask with dead eyes staring out at me. He releases his hold on my arm and I walk away into the crowd. I don't look back.

Pushing my way into the restroom, I put the drinks on a ledge by the sink and splash some cold water on my face. My reflection in the mirror is ghoulish, the fluorescents highlighting the grey pallor of my skin and the jaundice stain of my eyes. Lookin' good buddy. How the mighty have fallen. I think if Sarah met me right now, she wouldn't recognise me. I don't recognise me. But that's the point isn't it? Old Jacob wouldn't have the stomach to follow through. Old Jacob would be torn apart by guilt and his moral convictions. Old Jacob would say that all Sarah would want is for him to grieve, to accept that things happen for a reason and we must rise above it. The old Serenity Prayer comes to mind, the mantra of my diseased brothers and sisters. 'God, give us the grace to accept with serenity the things that cannot be changed, Courage to change the things that should be changed, and the wisdom to distinguish one from the other.' As I empty my glass it occurs to me the irony is rich, that I call on Dutch courage to steel myself against the echoes of my former life.

I prop up the bar for a spell, getting my head together. After a while, refreshed and emboldened with spirit, I come across Sofia in one of the smaller rooms, dancing with a tall black girl. She's strikingly beautiful with high cheek bones and silken chocolate skin, a criminally short skirt revealing long muscular legs. Sofia flashes me one of her sultry smiles as I lean against the wall and take in the spectacle. They dance close now, their hands on each other, gyrating as one. The music is the oriental haunt of the snake charmer with a heavy base rhythm. As their bodies slowly grind, Sofia kisses her, her busy tongue working deep inside. This erotic display combined with a head full of booze and dust is intoxicating. I stand mesmerised, the blood rushing to my groin. Sofia slips her hand discreetly between the girl's legs and begins working her fingers, all the time eyeing me with half-closed lids. My God, this girl is something else. She whispers something to her lover and comes to join me, leaving her conquest breathless and flushed on the dance floor.

'Hey *papito*, where have you been? I've been talking to some old friends. And making some new ones,' she adds, with a sly grin.

'Yeah, so I see,' I remark, still collecting myself after the floor show.

'Aw. What's up? Did that get my baby all hot under the collar?' she murmurs close to my ear, all coy like, while running her nails up my inner thigh. 'I see it did,' she says, finding me hard. 'No time now, *mi amor*,' she says to my disappointment, taking my hand and making for the exit. 'It's nearly twelve and we're going to be late for Raul's show.'

Truth be told, I'm not overly enthusiastic about the night's entertainment. Raul is one of Sofia's artist friends, a gifted Adonis with flowing black locks. Quite well known in these parts, his style mixes traditional Mayan imagery with bold contemporary stylings to create varying subversive political narratives. I have met him once before with Sofia. He was polite and attentive, but a whiff of condescension marred his tone. There was something in his demeanour which suggested he thought unfavourably of our friendship, perhaps because I'm a good few years older than her, or perhaps because he thinks I'm a dumb fuck gringo, here to rape and pillage his country. It could, of course, also be paranoia, a recent and disturbing addition to my repertoire of insanity. Each layer of acid onion peeling back to reveal more rotten meat, sour and darker the closer it gets to the core.

25

The cobblestone streets of the outskirts of town are hushed and poorly lit, the ghost glow of the street lamps creating spectres in the periphery. The clicking of Sofia's soft footfalls echo through the alleyways and off into the distance as we hurry on our way.

'This seems wrong. Are you sure you have the right address?' I enquire, a little irritated. The colonial style houses offer a grey face to the road, concealing their inward character. Often, heavy wood doors and dark stone hallways will reveal an eden of beauty beyond. Inside, quaint and colourful doorways spill out onto rustic courtyards rich with foliage, the air filled with the musical patter of water from a small stone fountain. I have always loved that about this town, a place of secrets. The timeless architecture of curiosity and wonder.

'Nearly there, baby. This should be quite exciting. It's not often Raul puts on a live performance, you know. It's mostly his paintings and sculptures that keep him busy these days. He'll be very happy that you could come along tonight.'

'I'm sure he will,' I reply, with thinly veiled sarcasm.

'No, I'm serious,' she reiterates. 'He told me earlier that he thinks you will especially enjoy the play. He says that you would have particular appreciation and understanding of the work.'

What the fuck? How does Raul even know I'm back in town, and since when has he taken an interest in what I like and don't like. This unusual development perplexes me, but also piques my curiosity. I've never been a great judge of character, so much so that I usually take my first impressions and assume the opposite will inevitably be revealed to be true. In this way, I consider myself by default to be an exemplary judge of character. By this twisted rationale, perhaps Raul is a stand up guy, and my initial conclusions were just a projection of my own feeble insecurities. Any which way, we've arrived at a door, unremarkable except for the fact there's no number and I swear there's no street name either. This combination of anonymous thresholds and the uniformity of the grid-like street design is hell for those of us without a sense of direction, and I rely on Sofia like a child fumbling in the fog.

Moments later, a short but stocky indigenous woman decked out in traditional dress grants us access, silently shepherding us toward a small doorway off the inner courtyard. A narrow stone staircase takes us down into a musty passageway, lit by candlelight from ornate fixtures lining the walls. As we move down the passage, the feeling of confinement is both oppressive and strangely exhilarating. It presently opens out into a round chamber, itself with many exits suggesting a network of stone catacombs, from which candlelit shadows flicker and dance. Despite the dark stone walls, the central room is plush and welcoming, with tapestries and intricately coloured weaves decorating the space, and a thick pile rug stretching the length and breadth of the room. Luxurious sofas and low oak tables furnish the room and antique shelves laden with piles of dusty books line the walls between each exit. A handful of people are scattered throughout the room, chatting and making merry.

'*Bienvenidos al Espejo, mis amigos!*' exclaims Raul, arms open as he approaches us. He envelops Sofia in a warm embrace, dwarfing her with his mighty frame, and murmurs softly in her ear, his speech too rapid for me to make out.

'And a welcome to you, Jacob!' he beams, embracing me roughly and clapping me on the back. 'I am very glad you could make it to my little *rendimiento*. Come, let us partake in a drink before we start the show,' he suggests, walking us to a small oak bar counter at the far end of the room. Raul strides across the floor, his long hair loose and falling to his shoulders. He wears a collarless white cotton shirt, open at the chest and trousers of a soft brown leather. I feel a momentary twinge of jealousy at his brazen masculinity and his rugged features, but it passes as Sofia gives my hand a small squeeze and tips me a wink. Encased shelves behind the bar counter house a myriad of decanters and tinted ampullas, each holding a promise of exotic liqueurs and byzantine spice.

'I have something extra special for my guests tonight, an interesting concoction for your pleasure,' he says, pulling a long stemmed bottle and three short, footed glasses from behind the counter. '*El hada verde*, or how do you say, the green fairy?'

Ah, absinthe. It shouldn't surprise me really. Ever since its popularity with the Parisian bohemian crowd in the early twentieth century, it's remained the inspiring elixir of the artist who wishes to commune with the spirits of Baudelaire and Toulouse-Lautrec. Its head-fucking properties have kept it firmly on the black list for many a year so I have yet to try it, but find myself fairly excited at the prospect.

'I myself, prefer to use *el método de la bohemia*,' explains Raul, pouring some absinthe into a shallow bowl. He takes three sugar cubes from a small pot and quickly dips each one in the liquid, allowing them to soak up the alcohol. He then fills each glass with a healthy measure of absinthe and, balancing a decorative silver slotted spoon on the first glass, sits one of the cubes on top. 'There are many who favour the French method, but I would never turn down the opportunity to avail of dramatic effect,' he smiles, as he sets the sugar cube alight and lets it drop into the glass, igniting the contents with a flash of colour. A shot of cold water douses the flames, leaving the absinthe with a cloudy consistency interspersed with hints of green. Raul repeats the process with each glass and then hands us our drinks.

'May you be in heaven half an hour, before the devil knows you're dead,' he exclaims, raising his glass. I admit to being somewhat impressed by his knowledge of this obscure Irish saying, and touch glasses in appreciation before downing the emerald nectar. The overwhelming flavour of anise is pungent and thick, and the potent juice has an immediate kick as the body and brain recoil at this affront to the senses. An intense heat emanates through my core and I rock on my feet for a moment, feeling a little lightheaded. Sofia is gasping slightly, her eyes watered and bloodshot. After the first wave washes over me, a feeling of crystal clarity and euphoria takes over, and I smile appreciatively at Raul.

'What did I tell you, *mis amigos. Magnífico*, no?' he beams. We agree whole heartedly, and after a few minutes of chatting, he leaves us to fix ourselves another, while he goes to prepare for the show to start. Shortly thereafter, the rest of the guests begin to filter out of the room through one of the doorways, so we take our drinks and follow suit.

A low ceilinged passageway leads us to a remarkable stone auditorium set deep in the ground, which is small and intimate. Four deep tiers are staggered down toward the stage, where a heavy red velvet curtain is drawn. The stone tiers are strewn with deep cushions in style with the previous chamber, so we find a seat and happily sink down into the comfort. There is a decadent, Roman feel to the place, and images of bloated aristocrats in togas being fed grapes by scantily clad servant girls flit through my mind. The room is dimly lit by oil lamps and the darkness is thick around us. As the audience goes quiet in preparation, I fight off a flutter of claustrophobia that whispers in my ear, and take a sip from my glass. The show is about to begin.

The curtain is pulled back to reveal two young Guatemalan boys working the land. They drag their rakes through the soil in unison, the efforts of their labour punctuated by the moan of a slightly discordant violin. The backdrop shows their small cottage in the distance, situated in the shadow of a tall fir tree at the end of the furrowed field. Presently, two hunched old women enter with glasses of water and approach the boys. As the mother offers the boy the glass and praises his good work, each sentence and action is mimicked simultaneously by their doppelgängers. This theatrical contrivance has a jarring effect, shifting the focus of attention between the characters and their mirrored counterparts. However, as the story unfolds and characters in the boy's daily life come and go, I find myself becoming accustomed to the presence of their other selves, and instead of distracting me from the story, it seems to enrich it with a whole new dimension and draw me in. The first act tells a pleasant tale of the young boy's life, long hours of toil, but innocent pleasure in the simple things; stealing a kiss from the neighbour girl, playing ball with his pals, an evening meal surrounded by a loving family and the comfort of a prayer as he kneels by his bed at night. At this stage

I'm captivated, entranced by the wholesome warmth of this delicately spun fairytale. I drink deep from my glass and sink down further into the cushions, cocooned in a hazy stupor. My limbs are heavy with a groggy weight but my mind is sharp and alive, the colours of the stage, vibrant and shimmering. I share the emotions of the characters, the strong bonds of their love and the wonder and joy gleaned from a life well lived.

The second act begins with a dusk setting. The lights are turned down low and the backdrop depicts stormy weather on the horizon. The boy is coming to the end of his working day when his eye catches something he hasn't noticed before, an orange tree growing tall at the far end of the neighbour's garden. The boy slowly approaches the fence, and stops, wondering how he has worked in his field every·day without seeing something this beautiful growing so close. The fruit is ripe and inviting, and the boy's hand absently moves to his groaning belly. At this point in the play, a curious thing happens. The boy's mirror image approaches the fence, while he stays rooted to the spot. This motion has an unusual dislocating effect on my senses. The boy climbs up onto the top of the fence and, straddling it for purchase, leans out and picks an orange. Climbing down again, he rejoins his doppelgänger and the boy, being whole once again, makes his way back to his cottage. The final scene of the act shows the boy sitting in his bed, feasting on the fruit, his bedside table littered with peel. Sated from his bounty, he drifts off into a deep sleep.

As the curtain opens on the third act, the boy is shaken from his slumber by his irate father. The father gesticulates wildly, pointing at the spent orange peels, fretting and wringing his hands. A heavy knock on the front door is answered to reveal two policemen, who subsequently take the boy into their custody while the boy's mother weeps and cries out. The piercing stabs of the violin are accompanied by a rumbling tremor on a base drum. The police are unnecessarily aggressive with the boy, one drags him by the hair while the other deals him a blow to the stomach. The raw violence of the scene is visited upon the audience twofold, as the players' mirror images echo the injustice. Dragged into the next scene, the boy is held upright while he faces his accuser. Raul stands tall and authoritative in flowing white robes, and gestures with pride to a large machine situated centre stage. The machine is a cubic contraption, ten feet high, with many moving parts. At this point, Raul and his mirror image become asynchronous, both moving to different parts of the machine to polish and adjust the calibrations. Preening enthusiastically, they highlight the different aspects of the machine for the audience, one shows the metal cuffs and shackles which hold the victim in place, while the other displays the whipping mechanism, which reminds me of a 'cat of nine tails' made from razor wire. All this time, the boy stands observing the machine, his expression passive and vaguely disinterested. It becomes clear that he has no idea he is the one being sentenced, or that the machine will be the punitive instrument in question. An ominous mood descends on the scene as many things happen at once. The policemen drag the boy to the machine and wrestle him into the shackles while he, realising his fate, kicks and screams in terror. At the same time, the mirror policemen walk the boy's counterpart slowly to the other side of the stage, where, as if in a daze, he takes Raul by the hand and turns to observe the proceedings. With his other hand, Raul throws a switch on the machine, and they both back away slowly, faces expressionless. I wince as the sound of moving cogs and grinding metal fill the theatre, and a flickering strobe light casts a nightmarish glow on the scene. The staccato of images shows the restrained boy's wide-eyed mask of horror, as the machinery builds momentum. As the whipping apparatus reaches top speed, its razor tongues begin to lash deep bloody fissures into the boy's bare back. The metallic whine of the machine grows louder and louder as the whips bury themselves deeper into the boy's flesh. Blood splatters the machine and the nearby observers, and chunks of flesh drop to the ground. His shrill screams and the vérité of the scene cause me to instinctively look away. When my gaze shifts to Raul and the boy, I feel my blood run cold. Still hand in hand, their faces are blank but their eyes burn into mine. Transfixed, I feel panic rise inside me, the sounds and images threatening to consume me. Just as the crescendo of noise becomes unbearable and I'm ready to surrender my sanity, it all stops. The machine is turned off, the boy's lifeless body hangs limp in the shackles, and a deathly silence fills the air. All the players are frozen as the lights are extinguished and a vacuous darkness cloaks the theatre. My breathing is still heavy and a thin sweat covers my brow when once again an amber spot-light finds the stage. The scene shows the boy in his bed, slowly emerging from the fog of sleep. He rubs his eyes with his fists, shaking off the dust of dreams, when he catches a movement out of the corner of his eye. He turns his head to see his mirror image sitting on a chair by his bedside, peeling an orange. As he slowly eats the fruit, piece by piece, his dead eyes stare deep into the boy's soul. Still lying in bed, the boy's eyes widen in fright as he sees himself for the first time. The curtain falls.

Lively applause and calls of 'bravo!' fill the room, as the stage lights are brought up. The cast form a line and take a deep bow, beaming in response to the adulation. The players turn to Raul and offer a special round of applause to their fearless leader, who graciously takes a second bow, humbly thanking them for this undeserved praise.

'That was amazing, don't you think, Jacob?' gushes Sofia, as the actors leave the stage and the audience gather themselves.

'Yeah, it was a pretty striking performance, all right,' I admit, regaining my composure and clambering to my feet on rubber legs. 'He definitely has a flair for the macabre.'

'*Si*, his work speaks to everyone, you know? The voice of his art is the one true voice, and most people are afraid to listen because they fear that which is inside them more than anything else.'

'Sure,' I agree reluctantly, just to keep her happy. I've never had too much time for this flaky bullshit rhetoric, art imitating life imitating art, ad infinitum. But I have to agree that the performance struck a chord with me. As we make our way out of the theatre and down the stone passageway, Sofia takes me by the hand and leads me down further into the catacombs, breaking away from most of the crowd.

'We should go congratulate Raul, no?' she says, dragging me in her wake. The absinthe is sitting heavy on me, and my coordination is shot. I try to grasp which direction we came from, but the candlelit passageways all look the same and I wasn't really paying attention in the first place. Fuck it. In for a penny.

We find Raul in what appears to be a makeshift dressing room, reclined on a chaise longue surrounded by his closest disciples. He's glowing from his performance and heartily invites us to pull up a cushion and join him in this den of hedonism. As Sofia fills his cup with praise, I take in the surroundings. The air in here is heavy with smoke and spice, and a lilting sitar melody dances through the room. The sound of chatter and laughter soothes my itching mind and, as I take a deep breath to clear my head, a tiredness washes over me.

'And you, Jacob. Did you enjoy the show?' asks Raul, handing me a glass of clear liquid. 'I find power in the ambiguous nature of symbolism. They are but tools to expose inner truths in men, simple keys to open doors. What is found on the other side is usually knowledge of one's self,' he smiles, leaning forward conspiratorially, 'or one's own destruction.'

I'm struggling to follow what he's saying now, and I muster some inane response, content to let the waves of fatigue wash over me. The panic of earlier has completely subsided, replaced with a warm and blissful state. It's reminiscent of when I was a young boy and I would fall down and graze my knee. My mother would take me in her arms and gently rock me back and forth until the sobbing stopped and, exhausted from tears, I would slowly drift off into sleep. Peace. Maybe that's all anyone really wants. Sofia is dragging deeply on the stem of a hookah, pulling the smoke deep into her lungs. She lies back with breath held, and then releases a plume of pink smoke into the air. She passes the pipe to me, her eyes large and swimming with pleasure. An attentive acolyte refills the clay bowl at the top of the pipe and gestures me to inhale. The smoke percolates through the water, cooling it and refining the taste. I fill my lungs, and pause before savouring the sweet exhale, the hint of cinnamon and cloves on my tongue. I sink deeper into the mist, as the voices around me float further and further away. Candlelit shadows play on the walls and the movements blur into one another. My eyelids surrender to the weight, and I'm pulled all the way down.

I come up for breath out of the fog. It's much darker now and it's hot, the air choked with sweat and electricity. My mind reels to grasp the moment, but falters each time, slipping on the oily surface of consciousness. I squint to make out figures in the dim red glow. Naked bodies undulate on the floor, grinding against each other like snakes in a pit. Groans of pleasure from ever corner, an orchestra of ecstasy. I feel myself getting hard and look down to see my clothes are off and a blond girl is fellating me, working her mouth slowly up and down. I can feel myself swelling inside the wet warmth, as her busy hands gently massage and fondle. The pleasure overcomes my confusion and I give in to it. She gets to her knees and lowers herself onto me, groaning in delight as I slip deep into her. Her eyes are closed as she gently rocks back and forth, absently teasing the nipples of her heavy breasts. I can feel other bodies near me, the heat of their skin. A hand caresses my arm, another, my inner thigh. She pumps her hips more rapidly now, finding her rhythm. I arch my head backward and catch the figure of Raul out of the corner of my eye. Sofia is straddling him but facing away, her eyes closed. Beads of sweat are visible in the red hue, trickling down between her small breasts. I can hear the whimper escape her lips as she bucks against him. Raul's eyes meet mine, and a burst of manic laughter fills the air. The laughter is wild and unhinged, the product of lunacy. It continues its shrill assault as I bear down, feeling the climax course through my veins. She takes me all the way. It is only the moment before I descend back into the darkness, that I realise I'm still laughing.

I pull into the driveway at the usual time and turn off the engine of the old Kessler sedan. I sit for a few minutes enjoying the quiet time. The calm before the storm. An ice storm. A landscape beset by chill and the numb blanket of silence. Things haven't been going well with Sarah for a while now, so much so that I strain to recall when things were ever good. I have it reduced to a couple of genuine happy instances in my head, but aside from that, our pain has worked retroactively to erase the past and rewrite it as a grim and ceaseless struggle. For Lily's sake, we've tried to avoid heated arguments and open aggression, but this has resulted in us opting instead for more subtle forms of weaponry. Scathing remarks calculated with precision to inflict the most damage. Emotional detachment is the name of the game and I experience brief moments of sour joy when I see how it hurts her, only to loath myself seconds later for feeling that way. I still love her with all my heart, but we have become so unkind to one another, that there is barely any energy left to mend what's broken. Ten years of marriage is a good portion of a life, and I sometimes feel that ending it would be like admitting you made a mistake that cost you over a decade, and so we stubbornly push on, held in deadlock. It would be so much easier if there was a concrete problem that we could address, an indiscretion or a disagreement. Instead we have simply grown apart, fallen out of love, and that hurts all the more. It seems Sarah has made her move into the spare bedroom permanent and we haven't shared a bed in months. Although we have tried to maintain the charade in front of Lily, I can see the situation is taking its toll on her. Even a seven year old is not so oblivious as not to notice the oppressive atmosphere in the house. Lately she's become a little withdrawn, and spends a lot of time in her room playing with her dolls. It breaks my heart to see her react in this way, but Sarah and I both think that separating right now would be even worse for her. This is how it is at the moment. Home sweet home.

It's already dark by four thirty this time of year, and a damp drizzle blows from the east. I'm slightly later than usual because of all the papers that need to be corrected before the end of term. I hold my coat closed with one hand while I lean back into the car and grab a bag of chocolates from the dashboard. It's become a bit of a ritual for me to buy Lily candy on my way home from work each Friday. We have a little routine where she runs to the door when she hears my key in the lock and waits expectantly for her treat. 'Oh, sorry sweetheart, I forgot to stop at the shop on the way home,' I say, with a playful smirk on my lips. 'We'll just have to eat carrots instead.' 'Come on Dad,' she giggles, rifling through my pockets, 'I know you got me something!' 'Maybe next week, sweetie,' I continue, 'I think we have some turnips you can chew on instead.' At this point she's wrestled me to the ground and, finding the treasure, beams victoriously. 'I give up,' I say, as I get to my feet and sweep her up in my arms, 'I'm no match for you.' I walk with her into the warmth of the kitchen while she tells me all about her day.

The first thing I notice is the lights. Normally at this time of the evening the house is lit up like a Christmas tree, but when I open the front door, the hallway leading to the kitchen is in darkness. Also the quiet is unsettling. Usually the kitchen is a hive of activity, with Sarah preparing dinner, the TV blaring and the electric buzz of various appliances. 'Hello, anybody home?' I call out. I find myself being a little annoyed at the idea that Sarah didn't phone to say they wouldn't be home. Has it got to the stage where simple common courtesy is too much to ask? I hang up my coat and climb the stairs, turning on the landing lights as I go. 'Sarah? Lily?' The silence calls back to me. The door to the spare bedroom is almost closed over, so I rap lightly to see if Sarah's inside. Again, no answer. Flicking on the light switch, I put my head around the door and that's when I see her, her face frozen in horror, her dead eyes staring at me. I can't move, can't breath. The bed sheets are soaked in blood and her arms are twisted backward so she looks like a grotesque puppet. Gaping wounds cover her chest and stomach and shorter gashes pepper her hands and arms. I lunge forward, my feet heavy like I'm wading through treacle. Dropping to my knees, I touch her pale cheek. She's so cold and lifeless that for a moment I imagine it's not Sarah, but a life-sized doll with china white skin and rosebud lips. The illusion dissolves and all I see is the broken body of my wife lying before me. Lily! I burst out of the room screaming her name as I stumble down the hall to her bedroom. I throw open the door and my heart stops beating. She's lying on her back on the bed, her thin little arms by her sides and a pillow

*covering her face. I gather her frail, limp body in my arms and
rock her back and forth crying her name over and over. Lily.
Lily. Lily. Lily.*

    I wake with a start, a sheen of cold sweat coating my skin and
the damp bed sheets in a tangled heap by my feet. Gasping for
air, I try to wrestle down the jackhammer in my chest, my mind
still skating the blade that seperates the conscious from the
gloom. The memories that elude me while awake bleed into my
dreams with more detail as time goes by. My conscious mind
hides from the memory, cowering in a corner with knees pulled
tight to its chest. It fears the truth would tear through its core,
leaving an ashen ghost in its wake to crumble in the wind.
Instead, my unconscious revisits that night time and time again,
tentatively filling in the pieces. I can still feel the picture is not
yet complete and that fresh horrors lie in the soft edges. A part of
me itches for the truth, to tear at it like a rabid animal, but the
coward in me is content to drink down the slow trickle of poison.
Although it sickens me to my stomach to keep coming back for
more, it still keeps me from dying of thirst. Ever since I was a
young boy I've always remembered my dreams on waking. Not
just jumbled images, but details, characters, colours, emotions
with crystal clarity. When Caleb and I shared a room as
youngsters, he used to pester me each morning to share parts of
my dreams with him, giving him access to a world that he only
knew as nothingness. Our mother used to joke that Caleb was a
dream chaser, starved of his nightly escape he would endeavour
to forge dreams in reality, a manipulative mage, blurring the lines
of the real and unreal. This playful conceit began to sour with the
years, as it became clearer that Caleb's inability to separate the
two was slowly tearing at the fabric of his sanity. For my part,
the world of my dreams was as real to me as the waking world,
so I embraced the stability and immutable nature of everyday
life. The anxiety started in my late teens. I would awake in a state
of panic, the feeling that I was trapped, unable to breath, clinging
to me with a vice-like grip. As the years went by I began to
understand the nature of my fear. The clarity and recall of my

dreams left me no respite from consciousness, in effect leaving me no escape from myself. Is refection, this is the point when I started to seek other ways to quiet my mind. If I couldn't shut it off completely, I would at least numb myself to the point of restful darkness. It was sometime then when I truly fell for my lady love, whose kisses promised oblivion that no other lover could. When she's gone, all she leaves behind is cold emptiness, but she always returns and holds me close, whispering softly that everything's alright.

Sofia's snoring rouses me from my thoughts, and I look over at her, her mess of hair concealing most of her face. The abandon of her bovine snorts brings a smile to my lips, this petite nymphette sleeping off last night's indulgence. I kiss her lightly on the arm and drag myself to the sink for a tall glass of water, my gums are swollen and my throat parched. I'm mildly surprised that we made it back to Sofia's apartment but considering the alternatives, the outcome is favourable. I take stock of myself, something of a ritual these days. I inventory my aches and pains, prescribing each one with its own remedy; codeine for my pounding skull; ant-acids for my putrid guts; alprazolam and a smoke for the heebee geebees. The tremors have also begun, unnoticeable at first, but as they build they're joined by other well known assailants, disorientation, confusion, paranoia. I count down the clock in my head, the fever sickness just strokes away. I'll pass by Kelly's on the way home and get the reckoner, that'll straighten me out. I pull on my clothes and make for the door, feeling around for my wallet in my jeans. Pulling out a clutch of notes, I peel off the usual amount and place it in a bowl of small coloured pebbles on the hall table. On my way out I close over the door as quietly as possible so as not to wake her.

'Gotta drain the snake, old chap,' says Lucas, climbing down from the barstool and trotting off to the pisser. 'Don't try any funny business while I'm gone. I've got a photographic memory, you know,' he adds with a smirk. I study the chessboard in front of me and work through a few possible strategies in my head. I have no illusions about winning the game, that would be a fool's errand, but there is something therapeutic about the structure of play. The skill is in envisioning the consequences of each action and extrapolating how these consequences can be manipulated to better your own position. Lucas informs me that it's the moves you don't make that reveal all to your opponent. I'm quite happy to play grasshopper to his sensei and it provides a welcome diversion in these lazy afternoons. I light a smoke and lean back on the bar. Finn is curled up by the foot of the stool in a fitful slumber, twitching and growling at whatever phantoms his canine mind has conjured. It's been weeks since I asked Pedro to set up a meeting with Uri but apparently he's been out of the country on business. My gaze shifts to a simple wooden door at the far end of the bar, the entrance to the back room where I first encountered that fucking snake. It feels like a lifetime ago that I sat in that room, shaking in my boots while Uri leered at me from behind his desk. 'The family resemblance is uncanny,' he grinned, menace seeping from every pore. 'And what, my dear boy, does a person like you have to offer a person like me in return for giving you what you desire?' What indeed. My answer brought a wolfish smile to his face, his teeth all the more prominent due to far receding gums. I would guess Uri's age as somewhere in his mid sixties, but he emanates the authority of a man who has earned his position with Machiavellian zeal. His accent has a faint Slavic whiff but his English is flawless, the softness of his tone only adding threat to his words. His head is always shaved clean, rendering his jet black eyebrows even more striking as a weapon of expression. He is clearly a man who likes to be well dressed and is always seen wearing a sharply cut white suit with a white shirt open at the collar. His cologne is thick and pungent like overripe fruit, the meat loose and swollen. On the occasions I've had the displeasure of meeting with him, there is always a young man in tow. He favours local youths with feminine features and a smooth jaw, who wait on him and cater to his whims. These encounters with Uri leave me feeling nauseous and dirty. I look forward to the day when our arrangement comes to an end but I fear I've simply become a pawn in a game I don't fully understand. I have become the unwitting servant in a war that time forgot, and whose kings have already left the battlefield.

'Penny for your thoughts?' enquires Lucas, sitting back down beside me while polishing his glasses with the corner of his shirt.

'Aw, just thinking about the first time I came here. Seems like forever ago.'

'Yeah,' agrees Lucas, 'time does tend to stand still in this place. So where were we? You were going to tell me the story of how you and Sarah met. High school sweethearts, I imagine, passing love letters and tugging on her pigtails?'

'Not quite so cliché,' I conceded with a chuckle, 'but close enough.'

I take a sip of my beer and go quiet for a moment, trying to find a good place to start. The threads of the past are so tightly knitted together that it becomes almost impossible to pick at one strand without the whole fabric coming undone. Lucas knows well enough what brought me here and what drives me to my goal. He has been my crutch on many a sodden night when, in my stupor, I rant and howl at the moon. The truth however is never that simple. The drink allows the blinders for the cries of righteous indignation, but the sobering light of day reveals the hypocrisy that bubbles beneath the surface, and that is why most men scurry back into the shadows at break of dawn. I have promised Lucas the whole story, for what it's worth. He sees the reluctant expression on my face and leans in close.

'I know you have regrets, Jacob,' he says, in a hushed tone, 'but that's the nature of living. The only respite we can wish for is to accept the past for what it is, and with clear eyes acknowledge sorrow and regret for what they are, simply experience. Thoreau put it best; 'To regret deeply is to live afresh.' Look around you,' he suggests, leaning back and considering the clientele who litter the bar. 'How many people in here are choking on regret? Regret for things they did or for things they didn't do, it doesn't make a difference. Most of them are paralysed by past regrets and fearful of the future because of it. So much so that they live in limbo, afraid of who they were and afraid of what they could be. It's that complacent nature of regret that keeps its captives mired in the fog until they become nothing more than ghosts.'

I scan the faces of the people and, for a moment, see them with new eyes. The undead, who have fallen between the cracks of life, out of step with the rhythm of the living. The pallor of their skin is faded and transparent, their cheeks gaunt and sunken. I recognise the mark of the forgotten, I've seen its reflection stare back at me. As quickly as it came, the illusion dissipates and the sounds and bustle of the afternoon pleasantries fill the air.

'So,' continues Lucas, straightening up and fixing me with a broad smile, 'as you were saying?'

I light another smoke and, running my hand absently against the stubble on my cheek, I cast my mind back.

'As I told you before, back in the real world I worked as an English professor. My father had been a columnist for the Daily Post and, though I think he would have been happy with any career direction I chose, he was delighted when I was applied to the language department at Trinity College. Like I said, Caleb and I were chalk and cheese, but still we were never far apart from each other when we were teenagers. As usual, he ended up with as good grades as I did leaving high school, but with minimum effort. My nose would be in the books every night, while he was out drinking with his mates or having a sly joint in the back garden. In the end he decided on Trinity as well, and over the course of the first year he bounced around from subject to subject, never sticking with anything long enough to make it through a whole term. But that was Caleb, you know? Anyway, it turned out that we had one Classical Literature class together, and that was when we both met Sarah. I have to point out that ordinarily me and Caleb didn't go for the same type of girls. The one or two girlfriends I'd had to date were quiet girls with blushing cheeks and shy eyes, who made sure I did my time before getting inside their pants. Caleb, on the other hand, attracted the wilder sort, pierced and angry and looking for a boy who laughed in the face of authority. Needless to say, their brazen disregard for behavioural norms saw Caleb get a lot more action than I did in those days. All the same, we both became infatuated with Sarah from the off. I remember sitting three rows up from her in the auditorium during some stuffy lecture. I couldn't keep my eyes off her. She had a thick mane of mousey brown hair that she always kept up in a high ponytail, and she usually wore a short tartan skirt, with thick black tights and heavy army boots. Her face was strikingly beautiful, with piercing blue eyes and full lips. Her skin was pale as the driven snow, but with a cluster of small freckles on each side of her nose. I remember spending many a lecture admiring her from afar. I'd look at the slope of her neck and imagine how it would feel to kiss it. I'd imagine how gorgeous she'd look naked, and how I'd love to spend hours just touching her.'

'Can I get you guys another round?' interrupts Pedro, sidling up towards our end of the bar.

'Yeah, go on then,' says Lucas, as he racks up some shots of Old Duke and a couple of ice cold Gallos. I drain my whisky and continue.

'She was one of these girls that exuded confidence, a sort of comfort in her own skin that was well beyond her years. The first time I talked to her she looked at me with those steady, intelligent eyes, and I swear to God she had the measure of me directly. It was like she saw through to the real me, even though I still hadn't found the real me yet. She had no time for the posturing and bluster of young men, so those she didn't scare off directly, fell head over heels in love with her. Sarah was involved in a lot of different organisations, human rights groups, environmentalist movements, that kind of stuff. In the end, this informed the direction she chose as a career, but at the time, she was quite the young radical. Sarah didn't subscribe to the conventional idea of a couple. She considered it, how did she put it, 'the institutional subservience of women by an archaic patriarchal society'. The idea of being in a relationship where you were faithful to one guy was tantamount to being his property. For her, she was a free agent, and if she chose to sleep with a guy, that didn't imply more than them sharing each others bodies for a night.'

'I can tell you really got on board with that idea,' quips Lucas, with a sly grin.

'Yeah,' I answer drily, 'I was over the moon. Anyway, needless to say, I fell for her. On the night of the first Fresher's Ball, we made out in the shadows behind the Science building. It was a warm September night and the noise of the party was humming in the distance. I had a full head of booze, and she wasn't far behind. She had a sexy, mischievous glint in her eyes and she rubbed up against me, moaning softly when I slipped my hand under her skirt. I remember she was a great kisser, very skilful compared to my experience. It was the most erotic moment of my life up to then. But I digress,' I say with a laugh, shaking off the memory and righting myself with a pull on my beer.

'So, it turned out she saw something she liked in Caleb as well. It never occurred to me that he was also besotted, but as time revealed, he was fixated by her. There was a Christmas party in the residence halls that year, a real rager. The place was wall to wall with drunken lunatics and everyone was full of seasonal spirit. At some point I crashed out on the couch, one shoe off, drooling on myself. I woke up a few hours later with a bad head on me, the room was grey with that sick early morning light. Only a few bodies were left, flaked out in corners, and the smell of stale beer and smoke was rank. I heard the creak of one of the bedroom doors and saw Sarah tiptoe out, dressed in nothing but a t-shirt three sizes too big for her. Her make-up was all smeared and she carried her jeans and shoes in her hand. I'll never forget the expression on her face when she noticed me lying there. I didn't understand it at first, it was so peculiar and conflicted, but then I recognised the t-shirt. It was red with a big black star on the front, just like the one Caleb had got a few weeks back.'

'That's rough,' says Lucas, sucking in air between his teeth, 'I guess you were pissed off with them both.'

'Well, that's the thing, you know, I had no claim on Sarah. We weren't an item or anything, and she had made herself very clear where we stood. And I couldn't really be that annoyed with Caleb considering I had kept pretty quiet about the crush I had on Sarah. All the same, it cut me deep. Unfortunately, the rational side of the brain is seldom congruent with the emotional side. I confronted Caleb about it later that day, fully expecting him to laugh it off, telling me it was just a bit of fun and I shouldn't get so worked up about a girl, but instead he looked me in the eye and told me that he was serious about a girl for the first time in his life. I was pretty thrown by this revelation. I had built up a good head of steam and then I find out he's just a love sick fool like me.'

'So there it was. Over the next few months we both pursued her, and things became a little tense between me and my brother. I knew she spent a lot of time with Caleb, but over the course of the year I felt that a bond had grown between us. It was like she was softening, allowing me to see parts of her that were private and vulnerable. Ironically, I was better equipped to play suitor than Caleb. He was used to attracting women, effecting that nonchalance and brutality that many women are drawn to and view as a challenge, bad boy made good by the love of the right woman. Back then he had this mop of curls and bushy sideburns and was a sight striding across the quad in tight jean flares and a vintage leather jacket. I wasn't a bad looking lad myself, but you know how it is at that age, it's all confidence and arrogance, and this came effortless to Caleb. So when it came to chasing Sarah, he just didn't have the softer touches or perseverance needed to win her over. On the best of days, Caleb had a temper, flying into rages at the drop of a hat or brooding in a corner, but as Sarah's affections became more focused on me, he became increasingly frustrated and sullen. It wasn't simply jealousy either. This was at a difficult time in Caleb's life when we began to notice changes in him, and the situation with Sarah played to his darker sides.'

I pause for a minute and take a swig of my beer, thinking back to those days. The once raw memories have healed over with gnarled scar tissue, but it surprises me the ease in which revisiting those times slices open the wound afresh.

'Caleb and I still lived at home at the time. That's the way it was back then, there was no way you could afford to go to college and live on your own, so you just had to knuckle down and do the work. The environment in the house was suffering from the rift between myself and Caleb, and my parents were becoming increasingly concerned with my brother's behaviour. As I said, his moods were always erratic, but there had become a marked difference in him in the last few months. It was usual for him to be easily distracted by things, but he became so unfocused it was impossible to engage him in conversation for more than a minute or two. For a lot of the time he exuded this nervous energy which, I could tell from the thin walls in our house, kept him up most nights. My parents tried to communicate with him, to gauge the seriousness of the problem, but he had thrown up a wall around him, reinforced by the concoction of booze and pills that had become his daily staple. This however, was not the worst of it. He also had periods of dark depression, where he would stay in his room all day or disappear from the house for weeks at a time. These episodes were hardest on my mother, as the overwhelming sadness visible in Caleb was breaking her heart. When she forced a confrontation he would lash out, a litany of venomous abuse, each word cutting deeper into ˪

'Some things that are said just can't be unsaid,' nods Lucas, exhaling a plume of cigarillo smoke into the air.

'That's the thing,' I agree. 'The more you love someone the easier it is to hurt them and that's a hurt that you carry inside you for a long time. Caleb knew this as well as anybody, so the guilt that he felt after these outbursts would threaten to consume him. He loved our mother more than anything in the world and it crippled him to see the toll it took on her. By all accounts my mother was a strong woman, stronger than most. She was born and raised in the north and, before she moved down to Dublin and met my father, she had seen and experienced the troubles up close. Which I can tell you goes a ways to toughening your hide. Anyway, Caleb dropped out of college when I was half way through my second year and moved away from home, for our mother's sake as much as his. He got a small bedsit in town and some shitty factory job to pay the bills and slowly but surely we lost contact with each other. Do you have any brothers Lucas?'

'No, not me, I'm afraid,' he says, with an air of melancholy. 'Once upon a time there was someone I could have called brother, but as fate would have it our paths led in opposite directions. I still miss him though.'

'Well, the space left by Caleb was a vacuum that ate away at my very being. All my life it had been me and him, side by side, facing whatever shit life threw at us. It was as if I was off balance, half a man. I kept trying to see him but it's difficult to keep up the effort when someone clearly wants to be left alone, and each time he spurned me it caused me pain. In the end, a whole four years passed before I saw him again and he had changed dramatically in that time. It was actually at me and Sarah's wedding. Yes,' I say with a smirk, 'in the end I managed to wear her down, even though it took a while. You can imagine how happy I was that he actually turned up, but it soon turned to shock when I saw him. For you to understand properly how he got to that place and, why he ended up doing an eight year stretch in Mountjoy prison, you need to know a little more about our mother's past.'

I notice a change in Lucas' expression, as his eyes move to the door over my left shoulder. Instinctively, I turn to see what's caught his attention, and clock Uri slithering his way toward us with a hermaphroditic youth in tow. I can feel a tangible change in the atmosphere in here, and the other afternoon punters blench almost imperceptibly with his arrival. The level of chatter drops off a few degrees and one or two of the stool monkeys steal cautious glances through narrow eyes. He comes up beside me and places his hand on my shoulder, his pale flesh offset by vulgar, incrusted rings. The sickly sweet musk of his perfume fills my nostrils and he looks down his nose at me like I'm a plate of carrion.

'How are you doing, my boy,' he asks, the weight of his touch still sitting uncomfortably on me. 'Not disturbing you I hope,' he adds with a vile sneer, which elicits a shrill, maniacal giggle from his boy. I reach for a smoke and paw around for a light as an excuse to extricate myself from his grip. Lucas and Uri give each other a reluctant nod. I'm not aware of the story between them but there is, without a doubt, no love lost.

'Let's talk in the back room, Jacob,' he says, returning his attention to me, 'I have another job for you.' On this note, he heads across the bar and, unlocking the heavy wooden door, enters with his boy and leaves it slightly ajar for me to follow.

'I guess we'll take the rest of that story some other day, then,' I suggest, turning back to Lucas with a sigh.

'I'll be around,' he answers, with a weary smile.

I slide off the barstool and crush the butt of my smoke in the ashtray. Polishing off the bottle of suds, I walk over and slip in through the wooden door, closing it firmly behind me.

'It's okay, Polina,' whispered Ölle softly to the terrified girl who sat shivering on the corner of the bed. 'This is your home now,' he continued, leaning in to brush a lock of lank hair from her face. The girl flinched from his touch, and a silent tear rolled down her cheek as her thin arms hugged herself for warmth. It's not often these days that he gets involved in this side of the business, but he misses the face time, the one on one. He sat down beside her on the bed and put his arm around her quivering frame.

'Andrei said you were causing a bit of trouble earlier, upsetting the other girls?' asked Ölle, eyeing the crimson swell around her left eye that had already began to yellow. He told those fucking monkeys to avoid the face because it turns off the customers, but it's hard to get it through their thick skulls. Shit, even with her knocked around a bit, she was still a nice piece of ass, sixteen or seventeen years old maybe. Still popular, these Russian girls, he mused, still top of the list for the clients.

'You need to take advantage of your situation here, Polina. Sweden is a country of opportunity,' he explained. 'Now this is a business like any other business, we've got to make money to keep afloat. Who's meant to cover the transport costs for bringing you here? How do you think my employees get paid? Do you think it's cheap to organise your papers and permits and also keep you fed and a roof over your head?' The girl shook her head, staring up at him with those big brown eyes. Fuck, I'm going to enjoy tasting this one, considered Ölle.

'I promised you a job, didn't I?' he goes on, softening his tone and fixing her with a warm smile. 'I have a position for you all ready to go, working in housekeeping at a big hotel in town.' Ah, there it is, he thought, the flicker of hope that they all cling to for dear life. It's proven to be the most effective tool over the years, the perfect companion to brute force and intimidation. When they lie in the dark at night and feel the cold jaws of fear clamp down on their hearts, the slightest whisper of hope will keep the madness at bay. If I just get through this then everything will be all right, they think. Pitiful whores.

'So all you have to do is stay here for a few weeks until you've paid off what you owe me and then you can start your new life, okay?'

The girl attempted a feeble smile, a slight quiver in her bottom lip, but her eyes still betrayed the paralysing fear inside her. That's the ticket, compliance through fear. Ölle lifted himself off the bed and made his way to the dresser where he had placed the box. The room was sparsely furnished with blank walls, except for just over the bed where a faded print of a mountain vista hung. Catching himself in the mirror, he absently clapped his expanding gut. Not a young man anymore, he thought, his blond hair and goatee streaked with grey and the jowls of his cheeks doughy and loose. Opening the box, he removed a syringe and placed it on the dresser to the side. He then removed a small sachet of brown powder and a burnished cooking spoon from the kit and, holding the spoon steady, began to carefully tap the contents into it. The expanse of his bulk shielded the proceedings from Polina, who now strained to glimpse what dark arts required Ölle's focus. The muscles of her thin arms and neck were tensed and her eyes wild, giving her the feral look of an animal who can smell the hunter coming but can't quite pick him out amidst the shadows. Sensing her distress, Ölle glanced over his right shoulder.

'Now, Polina. You know that I just want what's best for you. We're partners now and that means we look out for each other, right?' Polina nodded slowly but the current of fear held her body in its rigid state. Turning back to the works, Ölle flipped the cap off the needle with his thumb and, placing the tip in the spoon's bubbling concoction, began to draw the liquid into the chamber.

'It's important to get the right vaccinations when you travel from another country. I need you to stay healthy for me, because if you get sick it'll take a much longer time for you to pay your debts and start your new life, yes?' Another nod, this time a barely perceptible down shift in her agitation as she clung to the sweet promise of his poisoned words. Ölle held the needle at eye level and squeezed a few drops from the tip. That's the last thing I fucking need, he thought, her to die from an air bubble finding its way into her brain. I put enough time, effort and money into these whores for them to croak just as they're about to turn a fucking trade. This shit doesn't come for free either, you know.

Turning now to face her, he smiled the smile of a benevolent patron taking this young waif under his wing, offering nothing but warmth and protection. He sat on the bed next to her and placed a comforting hand on her shoulder. Moving in closer, he whispered into her ear, his breath warm and sour on her skin.

'Everybody needs medicine to stay healthy, even a beautiful young girl like yourself. Just leave everything to me, okay? You trust me don't you?' She smiled weakly and nodded, her eyes never leaving his, searching, pleading for a glimpse of truth in the mire, while inside she mocked herself for her weakness and naivety. You should know better than this Polina, she thought, chastising herself for her stupidity. But maybe, maybe if I just pay this debt I can start over and build a proper life for myself.

Setting the syringe on the bedspread, Ölle rolled up the shirt sleeve of her right arm past the elbow.

'Make a fist,' he whispered, as he held her arm out in front of her. Beautiful, he thought, tentatively running the tip of his finger over the blue veins that pushed to the surface beneath her pale skin. Picking up the needle in his right hand her gently hushed the whimpers that escaped her and slid the spike deep into her vein. Like a blade through butter, he mused, not like the ragged scar tissue of the junkie's perforated gristle, desperately tapping out the last healthy thread between their toes or genitals. No, this was the good stuff, virgin territory. Slowly he injected her, watching her intently as her heart pumped the payload through her body. The effect was immediate. Her eyes rolled into the back of her head and her jaw slackened, while Ölle lowered her back onto the bed. Every muscle in her body gave in to the rush and a moan of pleasure slipped through her lips. Nothing mattered anymore except being cocooned in this warm glow as it pulled her deeper into the depths of bliss. That's right, thought Ölle, massaging his cock through his jeans as he leered down at her. He leaned forward and ran his tongue up the length of her neck and into her ear, leaving a trail of dirty spittle on her flesh, discoloured by a ball of snus pocketed by his gum. Tastes like fucking strawberries, this one. He clambered to his feet and removed his leather vest, the saturated rings of sweat still visible through his black tee-shirt. His breath came short and laboured in anticipation of what was to follow. Again, he absently groped at his crotch and stared down at her, his pupils dark and hollow. Hiking up her short skirt, he ripped down her underwear and, after holding them to his nose and breathing in their scent, carelessly tossed them to the side. Her slight frame appeared all the more fragile as Ölle's lumbering mass towered over her. Spreading open her legs to get a better look at her, a salacious smile spread across his face, tinged with the ever present sneer of disgust. That's the money shot right there, sweetheart, he thought. That'll have the punters lining up around the block. Inhaling deeply, he drew thick phlegm up from his chest and spat a putrid wad into the palm of his hand. He roughly forced his fingers inside her, each feeble moan that escaped her getting him more wound up. Just like that, baby, you fucking love it. Finger after finger was pushed in until it could go no more. A few droplets of sweat trickled down Ölle's temple and his cheeks became flushed as the rigor of pumping his arm back and forth took its toll. Pulling out of her, he paused to consider a small patch of blood that had soaked into the bedspread beneath her. Shit, he thought, if I had of known she was a virgin I could have made a packet off of her. There are punters that would pay top dollar to crack one of these girls open. Just assumed a piece of ass like this would have been ridden senseless by the age of twelve. Oh, well. A whimper from the girl brought him back to the business at hand. Yeah, I thought you'd like your medicine, sugar, everyone remembers their first time. You'll be chasing that sweet taste for the rest of your days, he mused, lifting her limp, ragdoll body to the side of the bed until her head hung over the side. Prostrate and dangling off the edge, her eyelids fluttered open revealing only the whites of her eyes. A thin strand of saliva hung from the corner of her mouth and dribbled onto the threadbare carpet. Ölle climbed off the bed and hastily pulled at his belt, never shifting his eyes from the prize. Dropping his jeans and shorts, he shuffled clumsily around to where her head lolled, all the time working himself vigorously with his right hand. Now his breath came in whistled wheezes and his jowls had the ruddy hue of a bruised peach. Grabbing Polina's ears for purchase, he forced himself into her mouth, the wet heat eliciting a groan of pleasure from him. Even in her comatose state, Polina's body instinctively fought the assault, her throat gagging in spasm as he drove himself into her repeatedly. Just as he was working up to a climax, the poison in Polina's veins and the vigour of the penetration overwhelmed her, and a jet of acrid vomit erupted from her, drenching Ölle's groin and legs. Momentarily stunned, Ölle stared down at the congealed bile that had pooled in his shorts and jeans, his penis now flaccid and caked in filth. The physical barrage had somewhat shaken Polina from her stupor, and she sat up on the bed, groggy and disorientated, coughing and spluttering for air. Her mind reeled as she looked around her, struggling to make sense of the carnage before her, while the dawning pain she felt in her insides sent jolts of raw panic into her numb brain. Backing up against the bed's headboard and drawing her knees up to her chest, Polina stared at Ölle, wide-eyed and frozen. Ölle stared back.

A knock came at the door and moments later Andrei stuck his head around. A split second of wry amusement crossed his face as he took in the scene, but prudently readjusted itself to stony gravity as he addressed his boss.

'*Förlåt att jag stör dig, chefen*,' barked Andrei, excusing the intrusion, '*men vi har ett problem.*'

Across town, a figure made his way slowly through the dark side streets of downtown Malmö. The winds that whipped in from the coast barrelled down the narrow walkways giving a frenetic, tangible character to the night. The man was a stranger to these streets but moved with purpose, in synch with the architecture of shadows and in rhythm with the pulse of the cityscape. He was at once part of, but separate from, everything and nothing. The collar of his overcoat was pulled high and tight, concealing the lower half of his face, but his pale green eyes were visible, carrying within them the sadness of all the world. With his hands buried deep in the pockets of his coat, the stranger leaned into the wind and continued into the night.

Ölle hurried down a dimly lit corridor deeper into the recesses of the dilapidated building, while Andrei kept up the pace a few steps behind in silence. A quick clean up hadn't done much to brighten Ölle's mood, and Andrei knew well enough not to engage the boss man when his humour turned. This section of the premises was off limits to the punters and wasn't styled in the faux burlesque tack that adorned the front of the house, where considerations were made for the scumbag clientele's discerning tastes. Instead its walls were a shit green and flickering fluorescents threw a pale stutter down shadowed halls. Fuck, is this mess even worth the bother? thought Ölle to himself as they took a left turn into the bowels of the building. But he knew it was. He remembered the first time it happened, that Georgian bitch had managed to keep it a secret for nearly six months before he found out. You have to expect these things to happen of course, if a customer wants bare back he gets it, for the right price. Shit, most of these girls are barren from the pounding they get, their tubes all battered and broken, or from a venereal disease that chokes them up proper. Still, when one slips through you just send them to the Doc and in a week or two they're back in the saddle. It was different with her, though. Conniving slag said she was putting on weight, wearing those loose clothes, saying she was sick all the time. When we found out, the Doc said it was too late and other options had to be explored. Quite the fucking pickle. I remember talking to Per about it down at Mattsson's. I had noticed he'd gone quiet after I'd told him the situation and had a curious expression on his mug while he was sipping on his beer. 'You know, Ölle, times have changed,' he had said, fixing me with a look. 'People are more connected now, the world has got smaller, you know? Tastes have changed too. People who thought they were alone are now a part of networks that spread all across Europe and beyond.' 'What's your fucking point, Per,' I'd snapped, getting a bit impatient with his ramblings. He looked me bang in the eye, and lowered his voice to a whisper. 'Well,' he said, 'a man in your line of business could benefit from this expanding market place. There are people in this country and on the continent who would pay a lot of green to spend a bit of quality time with your problem.' True enough, after a bit of research and talking to a few punters, it turned out that these sick cunts would shell out their life savings if you facilitated their urges. Not my cup of tea, of course, but who am I to deny the will of the people?

Ölle came to the end of the corridor and pushed open the last door on the left. He was met with the anaemic wash of surgical lamps and the mother's primal screams as she cried out for her baby.

The stranger made his way across the square at Möllevången, passing by soundlessly, unnoticed by the night's revellers. The bars and restaurants cast their warm glow out onto the cobblestones but the light was swallowed by the cold shadows before it reached the huddled figure. The noise of festivities spilled out into the icy night air, and students wearing fingerless gloves gathered shivering under the outside heaters and passed a smoke between them. The rumble and screech of Turkish boy racers tore holes in the night as their muscular posturing left rubber burnt in their wake. A toothless old man with a scraggy beard and dishevelled clothes stood in the square, loudly proclaiming the end of everything to all who would listen, but no one would. He wore a faded wooden sandwich board over his front and back with some biblical scripture scrawled in red paint on either side. It read 'John 1:14, And the Word became flesh and dwelt among us.' As the stranger passed close to the fallen prophet, he paused in his rant and his wild eyes locked with the man as if in recognition. Moving toward him he shouted, '*Estus messodo divinius! Lexis etus silah!*' The stranger stopped in his tracks and turned to face the old man, an expression of mild confusion touching his features like a man being pulled from a deep slumber. Grabbing the stranger's forearm in a vicelike grip, their faces were now mere inches apart and the prophet's breath hung damp and rotten in the air between them. '*Estus messodo divinius! Lexis etus silah!*' he repeated, this time in hushed but urgent tones. A momentary flicker crossed the stranger's face, like someone whose heard a whistled fragment of a tune and can't quite place it. And then the moment passed. The stray mania returned to the old man's glance and he wandered off across the square, once more committed to his role as harbinger of doom. The stranger's gaze followed him, as his words and footfalls trailed off and were consumed by the night. Steeling himself against the rising wind, he turned and made his way down a narrow alleyway, its walls splashed with the pained cries of urbania. There was still work to be done this night.

'What seems to be the goddamn problem here,' barked Ölle at the doctor, who was hunched over a table at the far side of the room with his back to the door. The screams of the girl and the bloody rags that littered the room were having a jarring effect on Ölle's nerves and he wanted out of there. The girl was still positioned in the stirrups and was surrounded by some sparse pieces of hospital equipment and a high metal table with steel medical tools lined in a row. One of the girls who was called in to assist was attempting unsuccessfully to calm the young girl down, but she continued to flail and claw wildly, her body still coated in a slick sweat from the efforts of labour. Her skin, usually a deep ebony hue, was wan and sickly under the luminous glare, and the light accentuated the hollows of her cheeks and temples.

'Can't you give her a sedative or something, for Christ's sake,' yelled Ölle, over the din, his hand moving to his nose to stem the mingling stench of disinfectant, blood and sweat that assailed his nostrils.

'I've already administered a double dose, and I'm assuming you don't want me to kill her,' snapped the doctor testily, from over his shoulder. Don't give me any of your lip, asshole, thought Ölle to himself, as he crossed the room to join the doctor. Andrei moved to assist in calming down the girl. The doctor had been used on occasion for services such as this, but there was no pretence of affection between them, just a strained civility that periodically teetered into open hostility. Think you're better than the likes of me, do you? sneered Ölle to himself. Doesn't stop you borrowing money off me when you can't pick a winner to save your life, does it. The good doctor was in debt up to his eyeballs from the track and reluctantly did some work for Ölle in lieu of some heavy interest on his repayments. Ordinarily Ölle enjoyed watching him squirm as the conflict of his vices and pious moral high ground tore him apart, but today he wasn't in the mood for it.

'What's the situation,' enquired Ölle, as he stood beside the doctor, the two of them looking down at the frail body of the newborn, his papery skin slathered in clotted mucus and afterbirth.

'Couldn't save it,' replied the doctor. 'Its growth was significantly crippled by the amount of heroin in its mother's blood so that its lungs weren't developed enough to breath on its own. Probably better off that it died since the risk of cerebral palsy or retardation is quite high in these underweight infants. Maybe it wouldn't have happened if you didn't turn all these girls into junkies.'

Ölle fixed him with a cold stare, the promise of violence etched in his stance.

'When I want your fucking opinion,' he spat through gritted teeth, 'I'll ask for it.' The doctor deflated visibly, turning his eyes away and shrinking beneath Ölle's glare.

'So,' said Ölle, returning to the business at hand, 'get the girl cleaned up and back in a state that she can work again. And Andrei,' he continued, turning to the big Russian and gesturing to the table, 'you know what to do with this. Same as before, no trace.' By now the girl had partially calmed down and had been desperately trying to follow what was being said in Swedish between Ölle and the doctor. It was only now, with the last exchange, that the crushing reality of the situation hit home and a wail of grief burst from her lungs. As it trailed off into a whimper, her spent body crumpled back in the chair and her eyes glazed over. If anybody had been looking, they could have noticed that exact moment when all hope and the desire to live left her body, leaving behind an empty shell, hollowed and withered.

But nobody had been looking.

The stranger pressed on, the vibrance of the inner city steadily falling away as the thickening of the city's outer crust took form around him. Green faded to grey, individual footfalls echoed out like a cry in the dark. Life and the living had other things to do and the concrete graveyard lay still. Pools of neon from the street lamps cut through the darkness setting the stage for a play that everyone forgot. There was a muted desolation to these parts of the city. By day, office blocks and factories would teem with the bustle of industry and commerce, but as the sun set on the day, the walkways and side streets would fall silent. The ominous hush in their wake struck an eerie tone like an unfinished meal on a deserted galleon. The figure made his way across a parking lot and cut down a narrow alley which led onto a small back road. Arriving at a nondescript doorway, the stranger stopped and pressed a buzzer on the side of the heavy metal door. He turned his face to a small camera mounted above the entrance, his expression impassive, emotionless. After a few moments, a faint buzzer sounded and an audible click confirmed access granted. Pushing through the doorway, a few beats of thumping techno stole out in the cold night and were extinguished as the door swung closed behind him. Once more, the night was plunged into silence.

Ölle sat on a high stool by the small bar enclave in the common area nursing a large shot of Jäger and taking a moment's peace. The room was dimly lit by florid light casting a crimson glow on proceedings, while plush satin sofas lined the walls in an attempt to invoke a sultry charm to this house of harlotry. A gaudy facade to enable any romantic delusions of your average predator. The air hung thick and soupy, a toxic blend of smoke, perfume, stale beer and semen, and the constant throb of techno in the background filled the empty spaces.

He shook a smoke out of a pack of Prince, fumbled for a lighter and leaned over to grab an ashtray from the end of the bar. Fuck, he was edgy tonight, and it didn't really help with that baby business. Oh well, you win some you loose some, he thought, tossing back the shot and filling up the glass again. Unusually quiet tonight, though, he mused, throwing a glance around the deserted room. Some of the girls were entertaining guests in their rooms but it was still a slow one. Normally a few of the girls would be hanging out here, showing themselves off for the prospective punters or just sitting around listening to the tunes. At any rate, there was always something on the go. I could have sworn I heard Petra buzz someone in a few minutes ago, he thought, leaning over to drain the bottle of Jägermeister into his glass. As he turned back, a jolt of surprise shook him as he realised a man stood quietly in the doorway, his gaze taking in the measure of Ölle.

'Didn't see you there, *kompis*,' remarked Ölle, the tone of his own voice surprising him, like the dislocation you feel when listening to a recording of yourself. Shit, he was out of sorts tonight. 'You a first timer, or do you have a regular girl?' he asked, as the stranger slowly crossed the room toward him. No answer. Great, another fucking nut job, thought Ölle. You get every sort of psycho coming through here looking to get their dick wet. Still, that's the nature of the business. If they want something straight up they can get it at home, but here punters pay for the strange. A lot of them want to get in and out, no nonsense, quiet ones with shifty eyes and twisted minds. This one though, this one's eyeing me in a way I don't like too much. Ölle climbed down from his stool as the man approached him. He was no stranger to a bit of rough, so if this skinny cunt wanted some, he'd get some. As they faced one another, Ölle weighed in the stranger proper. Something was off with this, something that made him feel like a cold hand was gently cupping his heart, and he could feel the skin on his balls tighten. The man's gaze was mesmerising, both hazy and jaded, but at the same time it seared through him as if its point of focus was somewhere behind Ölle's eyes. An uncomfortable wave of nausea washed through him and unfamiliar emotions bubbled up from long forgotten depths. His mind clawed frantically at the insides of his head as he struggled to remember who he was and who he was not. The rhythmic thud of the base slowly ebbed away until all he could hear was silence, a silence so deafening and so complete that he thought his ears would burst. As the stranger leaned in close, it suddenly dawned on Ölle that the sadness in his eyes was love, and he began to weep like a child, tears rolling down his cheeks. The stranger's lips hovered by his ear and softly uttered a single word. A brief flicker of awe was the last Ölle knew before his dead weight collapsed in a heap on the floor.

It starts like it usually does. I'm sitting in the car, listening to the engine tick down until there is quiet, leaving only me and my thoughts. Outside, the whine of the wind and the patter of rain drops on the windscreen seem to echo my mood, providing an appropriate backdrop for my pensive state. Again, raw memories of young love and fresh feelings that have long since wilted fill my mind, and each time these memories become more vivid and nuanced, the hurt more real. How have we got to this place? How have two people who promised everything to each other, who gave themselves so completely, become the strangers who pass each other in the hallway, bristling as they almost touch. I don't recognise myself anymore and I don't recognise Sarah. We have become adept in the art of emotional camouflage, offering only what we want to be seen, while what's real gets lost deeper and deeper inside us. This mask of mine has become so natural and so instinctive that it has become almost impossible to tell where it ends and where I begin. I avoid eye contact with myself in the mirror, ashamed to look myself in the eye for fear that I might catch a glimpse of the real me, judging me, imploring me, despising me. And Lily. Sweet Lily. She reminds me so much of her mother when she was young, with those sparkling blue eyes and the same freckles sprinkled on either side of her nose. And her smile. When Sarah and I first got together, her smile used to fill me up. It was full of honesty and humour, not just her mouth but her eyes too. It was a perfect representation of what it was to be Sarah, all her goodness, her playfulness and her boundless energy for life, summed up in one expression. All doubts and insecurities would fall away when she would flash me that smile and, for that moment, the world was mine, because she was mine. Lily has that very smile, innocent and joyful, and when she beams at me my heart aches with love for my little girl and aches with sadness for old times.

I'm slightly later than usual because of the amount of papers I have to grade this time of year and, in my haste, I almost forget the bag of chocolates I bought for Lily on the dashboard. I lean back into the car, holding my coat closed with my spare hand as the wind whips and tousles. Fishing the keys from my coat pocket, it hits me that the house is submerged in darkness, which is unusual since Sarah should have collected Lily from school and been home a good two hours ago. Jostling the key in the lock, frustration mounts as my mind shuffles through reasons for this anomaly. Have I forgotten some previous engagement? Are they at her mothers and she forgot to call me? These days, irritation and annoyance seem to percolate close beneath the surface, boiling over at the first opportunity, and today is no exception. 'Hello, anybody home?' I hear myself call out. The silence in the house is total, and I feel the familiar twinge of self-consciousness that results from addressing the nothingness. Leaving the bag of chocolates on the hall table, I pull off my coat and hang it on the rack. I see Lily's winter jacket hanging on a lower peg, the red one dotted with small penguins holding umbrellas. I experience a small pang of concern that she's out in this weather without the proper clothes and, yet again, this quickly festers into resentment for Sarah's irresponsibility. But I admit to myself that Lily's wellbeing is always top priority with Sarah and so I make my way up the staircase to see if they're home after all.

'Sarah? Lily?' I call, after turning on the landing lights. Again, nothing. Rapping lightly on Sarah's bedroom door, I tentatively push it open and flick the wall switch. Horror turns my blood to ice water and I feel the chill spread through every vein and capillary as I stare into Sarah's blue eyes, now glazed and lifeless. My mind reels as I experience the moment in a

chopping sequence of mental snap shots, each one more horrific than the last. There is Sarah, limbs contorted and twisted, her body coated with sticky blood, far darker and viscous than imagined. There am I, kneeling by the bedside cradling her broken body in my arms, my face warped with anguish and despair. Time has frozen and nothing exists but this moment. There was no before and there is no after. Sobbing as I rock her back and forth, a small voice inside calls me back from the dark depths of grief, its watery call repeating one word over and over. Lily.

Staggering blindly down the hall to Lily's room, the smell of my own fear and the metallic stench of Sarah's blood are thick in my nostrils. My heart pounds in my ears like a jackhammer, so loud that the sound of me calling out her name comes from a distance, and the raw fear heard in that voice sends further bolts of panic into the pit of my stomach. Bursting through the door, I see her on the bed. She's surrounded by her dolls and teddies and there she lies on her back with her thin arms by her side and a pillow covering her face. Rushing to her bedside I gather her up in my arms and hold her as tight as I can, willing life back into her, but it's not to be. Her pale skin has already begun to blue and, holding her close, I can feel her cold cheek against mine, now wet and clammy with my own tears. Crying out her name, I rock her back and forth like I've done so many times, when the creak of the closet door behind me freezes me in place. Still holding Lily, I turn to see the silhouette of a man cloaked in the shadows. Watching. Waiting.

I'm torn from my dreams into the violence of the waking world, panting and dry heaving from the suffocating horrors of memory. This is how I wake nowadays, my sheets utterly soaked, my muscles sore from the tensions of the night. Finn eyes me with curiosity from his basket, one eyebrow raised in a lazy, quizzical expression.

'It's okay, buddy,' I mutter, not sure if I'm talking to myself or the dog, 'just bad dreams, is all.' This seems to appease Finn, and so he returns to his slumber with a weary sigh. The air in here is dry and heavy, a dense, unyielding heat. I crank up the fan to maximum and throw open the window a little further hoping for a blessed gust of wind, but nothing stirs this time of day. Parallel shafts of blistering sun cut through the gaps between the venetian blinds, the heat haze visible on the light that splashes across the floor.

I sit on the edge of the bed, naked and wounded, feeling the tremble in my hands and cursing under my breath. My head is thumping, brittle bursts of nerve pain exploding behind my eyes. I haven't always been this drink sick. Since Sarah and Lily died it's all I can do to lose myself. Once or twice I tried to lay off the booze but the sickness screams inside me, taunting me with visceral images that blend the real and the imagined into a feverscape of my own mad creation. Nerves, sinew, tissue, tear themselves apart in a fury of thirst so all consuming that many cannot be pulled back from the brink. Nowadays, the sickness hides in me, silenced momentarily by my habits, but the warmth of its rotten breath is on my nape. Like its nemesis, drink blurs the canvass, impossible now for me to know what is real or not, or even to muster the will to care. But if nothing, there is solace in the cool kiss of my lady love, comfort to be found in the soft edges, a faithful companion on this doomed pilgrimage.

I swig deep on a nagon of vodka I find on the floor by my bed, gasping as it hits its mark. I shake a smoke from a pack on the bedside table and, inhaling deeply, examine the glowing ember as it traces its way around the tip. Things have gotten worse lately. My only dream is not a dream but a fractured call from the depths of my subconscious mind, repeatedly filling in the gaps that my waking mind cowers from. Each night that I'm revisited by this memory, small details are added, meting out as much as my tender mind can handle without going insane. There has been a shift lately in these dreams, a slight dislocation in the events as if I'm becoming somehow more removed from myself as it becomes clearer. And there are changes, slight variations in how the dream unfolds, memories of emotions become skewed with repetition and in some cases turn to something entirely different. Before, I dreamed I was myself, experiencing the scene with fresh eyes, feeling everything for the first time. Now it is as if the dream has taken on a lucid quality, as if I am seeing myself reliving the episode, feeling everything second hand but with equal intensity. Where is the line between dream and memory if they are experienced as one and the same?

And what of reality of late? Where is the line drawn there? The memories of recent events lie somewhere just out of reach, and if I strain to grasp at their truth, these images are visited upon me through the filter of dreams. A constant sense of dread and panic accompany the haze of the experienced, flashes of cities I can't quite recall, faces that remind me of someone I once new. Memories built on shifting sands, interwoven in the fabric of my imagination. These conundrums cause me pain, head pain, heart pain, soul pain. A pain that cries out to be dulled, numbed, quenched.

I step out of the shower and towel myself off. By the time I've pulled on a short sleeved white shirt I'm already covered in sweat again. What's the fucking point, I ask you. I take a blast from the bottle before I go, trying to get a buzz on before I venture out into the afternoon sun. I don't spend much time in this pokey little flat. It's just a place where I can lay my head, really, a single bed, a small bureau and an on-suite bathroom and kitchenette. I usually take my meals elsewhere, but these days my appetite for solids has all but abandoned me and it's all I can do not to gag as I pass the food stalls that line the small streets. I feel this development has taken a serious toll on me physically and, fuelled mostly by liquor, the effort of simply existing tires me.

'I'll be back in a bit, buddy,' I tell Finn, putting on my shades as I get ready to leave. 'Best to stay out of this sweat, don't you think?' Finn snorts in agreement, and drifts off again. It's well for some.

The sunlight that white washes the walls of Antigua's streets and houses creates a blinding glare and, as I make my way into town, I hug the walls in search of a sniff of shade. My mood is dark today, my thoughts heavy. I cut across the square and head up Cinta Avenida Norte towards Kelly's to see if Lucas is about, as I feel his company would brighten my spirits. I haven't seen him since I got back and I owe him a story.

'So I'm there squatting over her, feeling a little self-conscious cause I look like a duck trying to lay a fuckin' egg, and it's just not happening,' says Johnny Boy, centre stage yet again with another classic tale from the memoirs of the depraved. 'And I'm puce in the face from the strain of it but I'm all backed up from a good few days on the piss, yeah? So she's lying there stark naked, and she looks up at me with these big puppy dog eyes that are startin' to tear up, and she says, 'What's wrong, baby? Don't you love me anymore?''

The punchline is followed by a volley of hearty laughter which brings a wide cheesy grin to Johnny Boy's mug. People shake their heads in disbelief, as they return to their drinks and their conversations.

A few beers in and a whisky or two in the hole, and I'm feeling like a new man. There's a good vibe in the bar today and it spreads throughout the crowd in jovial waves. Idly thumbing through an old paperback copy of a Sam Steward detective novel I find left on the counter, I pause to light a smoke and look around the room. Not a bad spot really. The bar itself runs almost the length of the room and corners in an 'L' shape a few feet from the far wall. A couple of high tables fill out the room, and some dark wood fixtures and faux stained glass fittings give a nice pub feel to the place. A wide stone archway leads two steps up into the second room, where long tables and wood benches line the walls. There's a quaint, ramshackle charm to the place. No leanings toward pretention, just an honest drinking house. The cursory nods to the old country are framed on the walls, the Proclamation of Independence, spectral portraits of Wilde and Yeats, rural landscapes of rolling hills. A dusty tricolour hangs lazily behind the bar and a stuffed leprechaun in a coffee mug screams 'Kiss me, I'm Irish!' There's a thrown together feel about the place that is strangely out of step with an intricate but faded gold leaf motif that runs along the borders of the walls and details the archway. There is an odd delicacy to the artwork that seems out of place in this sodden watering hole. My gaze falls on the wooden door at the far end of the other room and, just as the shadows begin to bleed into my thoughts, I see Lucas duck in through the front door.

'Salutations, all!' he exclaims, addressing the crowd as a whole. A murmur of welcome shuffles through the crowd and Lucas throws out a few handshakes and nods as he works his way over to where I'm perched by the bar. 'Jacob, *mon ami!*' he says, clapping me on the back and giving my hand a firm shake, wherein we exchange pleasantries and catch ups and get some beers in. Lucas seems extra buoyant today, sporting a crisp black cotton shirt and black slacks, he is the picture of eminent cool. He lights one of those thin cigarillos which I think make other men look effeminate but, with Lucas, seems to further accentuate his masculine ease. Tonic dropped and the spirit cleansed, we settle in as I pick up where I left off.

'Let's see, where was I? Right, my mother. Like I said before, Caleb and our mother were very close and they always had this unspoken bond with each other, like they were in tune, resonating at the same frequency. My father and I were also very close but they definitely had a special connection. Hindsight has a funny clarity to it, you know? As children growing up, our home life was all we knew, there was no frame of reference by which to judge what was normal or not. It's only when you get out into the world that you begin to realise that your parents can be flawed, that they are susceptible to the same shortcomings as anyone else. I think that's one of the hardest truths of adolescence. I think there is an automatic feeling of resentment that comes with that realisation, a feeling that you have been somewhat duped into believing your parents were perfect and the foundation of your reality and your sense of security has been built on a fabrication.'

'Anyway, as I told you, my mother was born in the north, in county Antrim. From a very young age, she charmed us with tales of old Ireland, its rich history and the legacy of our heritage. Our bed time stories were the mythical legends of the Fianna, a band of warriors who lived in the forests led by their fearless leader Fionn mac Cumhaill, and who were called on in times of war to serve the high kings. We were enchanted by their heroics and bristled with eager pride to thing that we were descended from such giants. Even before we were old enough to go to school we were already well versed in the Irish language and our nightly prayers were recited in fluent Gaeilge. There was no separation between religion and nationalism, to be Catholic was to be Irish and to be Irish was to be Catholic, and this blurring of distinctions imbued in our young minds a sense of righteousness. As we grew, our mother told us of the historical struggle under British rule and the atrocities visited upon our people. She told us how the rebel Volunteers, led by the great Padraig Pearse and James Connolly, fought for independence during the 1916 Easter Rising only to be spat on and stoned by their own as they were bound and marched through the streets of Dublin. These stories touched us, and the Fenian spirit went a long way to shaping our identity as we got older.'

'I remember when we were in fifth class, which means we were about eleven years old. We had a weekly assignment which was to write a poem and read it out for the class on Fridays. Each child rattled through the standard fare, poems about their pets or their grannies or football, expectedly childish rhyme and verse. When it came to Caleb's turn, he strode to the front of the class and began to read from his paper. As I said, Caleb was a gifted child, skilled and creative if somewhat erratic. His poem told of a mother, left to tend the land on her own when her son went off to war. It spoke of loss and hurt and the toll of oppression on the innocents. It told of the sacrifices that need to be made when the cause is just and it spoke of the eternal rewards in the life there after. It was a chilling poem, all the more striking due to its measured, mature tone. I can still remember lines from it today, filled with subtle symbolism and mystical imagery. The teacher was visibly shaken by the reading and muttered some confusing comments before ending the class. The following Monday, Caleb was summoned to the principals office during a lesson and when he returned fifteen minutes later, I was then called up. The principal sat grave-faced across the desk from me along with a serious looking man in a black suit and spectacles. In front of him on the table I could recognise Caleb's poem, his nearly illegible scrawl quite obvious even from that angle.'

'The principal began by asking if I knew if Caleb had written the poem himself and I answered that I assumed he had, even though I didn't witness the actual writing myself. He then went on to ask if our mother helped us with our homework often. I remember it being a very odd experience. His questions were carefully weighed and deliberate, after which his glance would flick to the other man as if to seek approval. The line of inquiry then shifted to our home life and questions regarding activities and friends of the family ensued. My young mind had no notion of subtext and the seemingly pointless nature of the questions baffled me, so much so that I shrugged off the whole experience the second I left the room. It wasn't until some weeks later, when rumours started circulating in the school yard, that I made any connections.'

'It started with a very simple word. Honeytrap. One of the boys had overheard his parents talking about our mother being involved in a honeytrap operation in the north, back before she moved down to Dublin and met our father. It was as much the exotic and mysterious nature of the word itself and what it conjured up in a young boy's mind that started the buzz going around the school. A honeytrap is a general term used mostly in espionage which involves a female operative using sexual seduction to achieve some tactical advantage. In Northern Ireland, during the worst of the troubles, there were recorded instances where a female member of the IRA would lure British soldiers back to a flat, only to be executed by masked men who were lying in wait. Needless to say, when these rumours found there way to our ears, Caleb and I were quite upset and confronted our parents about it that night.'

'That must have been an interesting conversation,' says Lucas, one eyebrow raised over the frame of his tinted glasses.

'Yeah, well it was definitely a night that stuck in my mind, even now it's still quite clear in my memory. It was perhaps the first occasion I saw my parents as individuals, separate people with different pasts and different opinions. I mentioned before that my mother was quite passionate and emotional, just like Caleb, and that my father was more introverted and rational, traits that I picked up in the mix. In the same way that I provided grounding for Caleb, our father was the soothing voice of reason during our mothers more manic episodes. When we told them of the rumours in school they both just sat there opposite us in silence and, after a few moments, our father told us to go to our rooms and wait there until we were called. We lay on our beds and listened to the heated argument that carried on below. The murmured exchange began to build and the raw anger was apparent in their tones. Although we couldn't hear the conversation we could make out the odd word and fragment as the argument overheated. '…why should I deny…,' came our mother's shrill voice. '… no right to impose your…,' barked our father. '…cowardice…', '…stubborn…', '…we said we'd never…' That kind of stuff. This was the only time we'd ever heard our father raise his voice and in those few moments they

69

both became something else to us. It was if we were instantaneously dragged into adulthood across a room of broken glass. Caleb wept quietly, his face buried in his pillow, and when the argument finally abated our parents came up to our room. Our father did most of the talking, saying that the rumours weren't true and that those people didn't know anything about our mother. He told us that it was just mean-spirited lies concocted by bored and stupid minds. All the while, my mother sat on Caleb's bed, his head cradled in her lap as she stroked the tears from his cheek. She didn't say much at all, just sat there, her expression numb, looking from me to my father and back again.'

'Everything changed after that. My mother became withdrawn and the bright glint that she always had in her eyes faded ever so slightly. There was a noticeable change in Caleb's behaviour as well. He craved a lot more attention from our mother, both spending an increasing amount of time together, and he became very defensive of her. By the same token, his attitude towards our father became cold, and although he was not outright aggressive toward him, there was an element of reproach in his manner. Like I said, that was a pivotal moment in our childhood and it was never talked about again between me and Caleb. I had all but buried the memory completely, but nearly a decade later, situations arose that brought it back to me with crystal clarity.'

'You boys need a refill?' asks Pedro, pulling two bottles of ice cold Gallo from the fridge and waggling them in our direction. Pedro is a mountain of a man, an El Salvadorian with muscular bronzed forearms and wiry jet-black hair. I honestly can't remember a time when he hasn't stood here tending bar.

'Hell, yeah,' replies Lucas, 'and I think we'll be needing a few shorts of that fire water as well. Hold that thought, Jake. I gotta go see a man about a dog,' he says, sliding off the barstool and making for the head. As I light up another smoke, I'm surprised to find how much these stories of my past leave me shaken and unhinged. I guess remembering how close we used to be as boys makes the place we've arrived at now all the more heart-breaking.

Absently scanning the room, I see Pedro at the far end of the bar gesturing for Johnny Boy to come talk to him. Something strikes me as odd about the exchange as Pedro leans over and talks intently into his ear. Pedro, who normally comes across as a good natured guy, if anything a tad slow, looks momentarily transformed. His eyes burn with glacial intelligence and his whole demeanour is distinctly authoritative. Johnny Boy's perpetual smart-arse grin falters for a moment and his boyish features assume the gravitas of a man twice his age. It seems to me that there is no fear in that look, just the dawn of some understanding. These days, episodes of this nature are common for me. Incongruent elements stalk my perceptions so that the ground constantly shifts beneath my feet. I find these ripples in everyday experience trouble me more than the elaborate horrors that visit my nights, leaving me mired in suspicion and doubt. A few final words pass between them after which Johnny Boy nods his head and makes his way across the bar. I can't drag my eyes from his face as he passes close by me, searching his expression for something recognisable but finding nothing. I imagine for a split second that he looks at me and his lips move soundlessly. What? I ask, struggling to understand, but I'm uncertain if I spoke aloud or simply thought I did. I watch him cross the floor to the far end of the bar and let himself in through the door to the back room.

'What's wrong, Jacob?' asks Lucas, putting his hand on my shoulder and pulling me back out of my head. 'You're sweating like a bastard. Is everything all right?'

'Yeah, yeah,' I stammer, pulling deep on my beer to quell the tremor in my hands, 'just a bit off to day, is all. It's more difficult then I thought to dredge up these memories.'

'You don't have to continue if you don't want, Jake,' he says, fixing me with a look of genuine concern.

'No, it's fine,' I say, the anxiety slowly subsiding. 'I suppose it's cathartic in some way, you know.' 'The cleansing nature of the confessional, and all that,' I add, with a wry smile.

'And I will hear your sins, my boy,' bleats Lucas, in one of the worst Irish brogues I've ever heard, making me almost spray a mouthful of beer all over the counter.

'Okay, okay, let's see,' I say, settling down after the laughter had subsided. 'There was that four year gap after Caleb moved out where I didn't see or hear from him.'

'By this time, Sarah and I had gotten a little flat together while we were both working on our dissertations, and I was already getting a bit of work lecturing the first year students. Sarah was picking up a few hours waitressing as well, but things were definitely tight for a while and we struggled to make ends meet. But for all intents and purposes we were as happy as two people could be. We existed inside of that cocoon where the sun rises and sets with each other, and life's worries are mere trifles when you know you'll spend the night in the arms of your lover. It was a haze of happiness that felt like being born again, like a veil had been drawn back leaving your senses tingling with the crisp wonder and possibilities the world had to offer. In the summer we would spend afternoons in the park across the street, lying on this tattered old blanket under a gnarled horse-chestnut tree we claimed as our own. I would read to Sarah from whatever poet or novelist I was interested in at the time, while she laid her head in my lap and lost herself in the shafts of sunlight that broke through the branches. I can still remember the smell of newly cut grass carried on the breeze and the texture of the tree's bark against my skin. In the winter evenings, we would bundle up in front of the heater and drink vegetable soup from coffee mugs. There was little or no insulation in those old buildings and Sarah's nose would be red and shiny from month long sniffles. We'd listen to old recordings of Will De Lue and Rosalie St.Croix while I'd role cigarettes and we'd talk long into the night about our dreams, unguarded, unafraid, like children. And when we'd finally turn in, we'd make love, drowning in each other like we were the last two people on earth.'

I pause for a moment, transported back to a time when I was someone else, and I feel my heart heavy in my chest.

'Nostalgia's a funny thing, Lucas. Do you know the etymology of the word? It's a compound of the Greek word *nóstos*, meaning 'returning home', and *álgos*, meaning 'pain'. Is it painful because it's a memory of something we lost? Or is it painful because it opens our eyes to the fleeting nature of things, a greater understanding of the passage of time? I really don't know, but it tears at me to think back to how happy we were in those days.'

'Most of us choose to view the past through rose-tinted glasses,' injects Lucas, with a wistful smile playing on his lips.

'Indeed,' I say, with a chuckle. 'Is any memory actually an accurate version of past events? I mean, memories only arise as a reaction to some line of thought, the nature of which calls upon a past experience within some causal framework. Therefore, no memory can be taken out of the context of whatever frame of mind conjured them up. They can only be viewed through the prism of all that came after. We rely on memory as if it were something concrete, unchanging, but it is shaped and reshaped but the subconscious, colored by emotion, sculpted by fear.'

We go quiet for a bit, take some drinks, smoke some smokes. Lucas looks lost in his own thoughts. My head is still in the past, in that small flat, with Sarah. Was it real? At least I think so. There's a reckless abandon to young love, before hurt becomes familiar and the foundations for the walls are dug. My mind skips ahead to the sober reality of our life years down the line when the intoxications of youth left us wincing in the cold morning light. We can no more promise our feelings for someone won't change than we can promise we will live forever. What are the whisperings of love but a prayer of hope muttered with the convictions of a true believer. And when the time comes for true love to fade and die, is it not a death of the self and a reincarnation in another form? A changeling, filled with new convictions and born in the ashes of what came before. The same injustice is felt by the lover as by those who are on death's door, when the reality of nature's ambivalence to there cries is crushingly and totally realised. Yet the world keeps spinning, and the quest for immortality rages in the heart of every man.

'You ever been in love, Lucas?' I ask, suddenly curious. Lucas has the unusual knack of talking incessantly without ever really divulging anything about himself. In some ways I feel I know him intimately, almost better than anyone I've ever met, yet in reality, I know very little about him. In saying that, there is an unspoken agreement amongst the souls who have washed up here that the past is past, and that's where it should stay.

'Yeah,' he says quietly, taking off his glasses and wiping the lens with a corner of his shirt. 'It was a long time ago, though, an eternity. I was a different guy then, full of passion and fire, the hunger of youth. But in the end it just became a battle of wills, grinding each other down until we broke each other's hearts. In some ways I think we were too alike, giving as good as we got until it spiralled out of control. After the dust settled, we'd simply nothing left to give, so we went our separate ways. Broken.' A few beats passed before he speaks. 'It's been a while since I've thought about that,' he says, clearing his throat and shifting his position on the barstool.

'So, then,' he says, brushing himself off, 'the next time you saw Caleb was your wedding?'

'That's right. Since Caleb had broken off contact with the family, things had not been going great for my parents. I tried to see them as often as I could, but between school and work and the little time I got to spend with Sarah, it wasn't a regular thing. The vacuum left by Caleb took a heavy toll on my mother which ate away at her. She was always vibrant and high-spirited, her shock of red curls and rosy cheeks would light up any room, but the last few times I had seen her she had looked washed out, drained of all colour. Her eyes were bruised with the weight of her loss and she looked smaller and more fragile, as if the wind had been knocked out of her permanently. My father was also in bad shape. He had suffered from a condition called retinitis pigmentosa for many years which was slowly but surely claiming his sight. It had progressed rapidly in the last few years from night-blindness and mild blurring to prolonged instances of tunnel vision which, for a man who made a living with the written word, was both frustrating and terrifying. Now that I think about it, on those occasions I went to visit them they were actually never in the same room at the same time. My mother was either in bed, or sitting at the kitchen table with a cigarette hanging between her fingers, staring out the window to the back garden. My father would be buried in his study, scribbling in his journal, his face about two inches from the paper. I'm not sure which was actually worse, my father's irritability and insistence that he didn't need help, or my mother's disengagement. Either way, in the end I found excuses not to see them and became adept at convincing myself that I just didn't have the time.'

'Like I said, after Caleb moved out I tried to keep in touch, after all we were brothers, twins for God sake, but he made it very clear I wasn't welcome. Still, I was compelled to keep tabs on him, and over the years I managed to pick up bits and pieces from common acquaintances, slivers of information regarding his well-being. These titbits did nothing to ease my mind, instead they acted as news bulletins charting his rapid and inevitable decline. Just before he disappeared off the radar completely, it appeared he was running with some undesirable types, and it was rumoured he was involved in illegal activities. Needless to say, I didn't share this information with our parents since they were already racked with guilt and worry. But what was I to do? Caleb was a grown man, big and bold enough to make his own decisions and face the consequences. Somewhere inside me, though, I felt bad about how the situation with Sarah had affected him, so I was over the moon when, out of the blue, he turned up at our wedding reception years later. But that joy was to be short lived.'

'Of course, if I had of known where Caleb was living at the time I would have sent him a wedding invitation, but he had literally dropped off the face of the earth. To be honest, there were other things to think about, what with wedding arrangements and the shit storm that comes with that. True to form, we were obliged to invite the whole fucking clan, great aunts, second cousins once removed, the whole shebang. It came together nicely on the day, Sarah looked radiant and the ceremony took place in our local church with the afters out in a nice hotel by the coast. Irish weddings are something of a knees-up, you know?' I say, grinning at Lucas.

'Why doesn't that surprise me, Jacob,' he counters, with a broad smile.

'So, the dinner and speeches and what not are over with and everyone's in high spirits, most people are up dancing or hanging in the bar and lounge. It's just a carousel of faces and truncated conversations, embraces and back slaps, well-wishers whispering in your ear as you're passed around the room. Every now and again, Sarah and I share a look across the room, stealing a moment from the melee, blowing me away with one of her killer smiles. At some point I go up to the bar, if anything just to take a breather. The round bar is an expanse of polished oak with a thick column of split mirrors at the centre where the liquor bottles are housed. I'm absently looking at the crowd through the splintered reflections, when my blood runs cold and my heart skips a beat. I see Caleb staring back at me, his face warped in the curvature of the glass. After the shock subsided and the ability to move returned to my limbs, I made my way around to the far end of the bar to where he sat. It was such a flurry of emotions, confusion, resentment, guilt, but mostly an overwhelming feeling of happiness to see him again. There was also alarm, a burning pit in my gut that began to grow as the minutes ticked by. Caleb did not look well. His black curls were gone, shaved down to a dark stubble, revealing a few pock marks and small scars around his skull. He was wearing a heavy wool coat, like a long shoreman's, and dark jeans with army boots. He had grown a thick goatee, which made it difficult to judge his expression. He was always easy to read, signposting his mood swings with a curl of his lip or the twitch of a grin, but he was masked now, giving nothing, like a coiled viper. I hugged him and he hugged me back, maybe too tightly.'

'Almost immediately, I could tell he was drunk, I mean really drunk. His eyes were bloodshot and he was more erratic then usual, slurring some words and seemingly unaware of the volume of his own voice. But there was intensity and focus in his manner that kept me constantly on edge. He congratulated me on my marriage, his tone shifting back and forth between genuine sentiment and bitter, poisonous sarcasm. I can't really remember what I said in those first few moments, my mouth was on autopilot while I searched his eyes for something I recognised. I was so engrossed that it was quite a while before I realised he wasn't alone, he had a companion sitting beside him at the bar that he hadn't even introduced, a weaselish fellow with an ugly mouth and mean eyes. He paid us little attention, just sat there sipping his pint and sniggering to himself every now and again, but his presence stilted my conversation with Caleb, stopped me from asking the questions I wanted to, kept me at arms length. Of course, I have no doubt that that was Caleb's intention, as for what he planned for this momentous reunion, I don't think he really knew himself. As we talked he appeared extremely emotionally distraught, as if whatever anchor was holding him down in the high seas had come loose, leaving him to thrash around at the mercy of the elements. One moment he would seem sullen and wounded and seconds later he would flash white hot anger, only to be apologetic and filled with remorse. I could tell by his gaunt features that this constant struggle was draining him, feeding off him.'

"I gotta go,' he had said, suddenly climbing off the stool, as if he had forgotten some prior engagement. That's when things took a turn for the worse. The anger just started to build in me. I thought to myself, how dare he just turn up here with this shabby fucker at my goddamn wedding after all these years, only to piss off again because he feels like it. I felt indignant, like I deserved some answers. It was so painful when he cut off contact before, and now he thinks he can just come and go as he pleases? 'Are you not even going to say hello to your own mother and father? Or congratulate Sarah?' I had asked, partially blocking his exit and putting a hand on his shoulder. I was surprised to hear the intensity in my voice, surprised by the potency of my own anger. Caleb stopped dead in his tracks, a brief flicker of disbelief crossed his face followed by a distinctly aggressive adjustment in his posture. I should have expected it really, Caleb was never the type to back down from confrontation, but I felt justified and determined to follow through. 'Get out of my way, Jacob,' he had said. 'Go back to living in your perfect little bubble with your new bride and leave the business of the real world to the big boys.' 'And what business is that?' I said, fuming now, and squaring up to him, 'breaking the law and fucking people over?' Caleb's eyes burned through me and he moved in close enough to feel the heat of his breath on my skin. 'You were always a self-righteous cunt, Jacob, always hiding behind your words because you never had the stomach for action. Always making excuses for your own cowardice with the lies you tell yourself. You're pathetic,' he spat, and made a motion to move past me, but his words had driven me into a frenzy of rage. I shoved him back hard with all my strength and he winced in pain as his spine struck the edge of the counter. At this point we had got the attention of some of the guests and a crowd was beginning to form close to us. Caleb came back at me fast, hitting me in the jaw with a clenched fist. I was momentarily stunned but managed to keep my footing, rallying with a solid blow to his ribs. After that we just became entangled in each other, stumbling around the room knocking over tables of drinks, clawing and grabbing at each other for purchase, throwing digs when the opportunity arose. I could feel the copper taste of blood in my mouth and a gash had opened up on Caleb's forehead and was smeared across his face like war paint. Everything was a blur. I could hear the shouts of people trying to tear us apart. I could hear the snigger of Caleb's shady companion in the background. I could hear Sarah screaming my name and my mother's anguished wailing.'

'When they finally succeeded in separating us we were held fast by a sea of arms while we stared at each other, panting and wild-eyed. Sarah stood to the side, tears rolling down her cheeks, looking from me to Caleb and back again. It's hard to say what I felt at that moment as I saw the look that passed between Sarah and Caleb, but there was something there that I didn't understand, something just beyond my grasp.'

'The bartender had pressed the silent alarm just as the first blow was dealt and it hadn't taken long for the police to arrive at the scene. Needless to say, Caleb's friend was nowhere to be found when the dust settled. Fingers were pointed and Caleb was cuffed and taken away in the squad car. I know what you're thinking, not such a big deal, right? We wouldn't be the first brothers to get involved in a bar brawl. Unfortunately, it was the tremor that gave way to the avalanche. It transpired that Caleb had been on a watch list with the Gardaí for some time, and when they searched his car after the arrest, they came across a stash of handguns and rifles in the boot. Then the whole house of cards came tumbling down. More weapons were seized back at the house he was staying at, and this was followed by more arrests. I can still see the headlines in the paper that week, it read 'IRA Gunrunning Operation Blown Wide Open', and had a picture of Caleb and his co-conspirators shackled on the steps of the high-courts with jackets thrown over them to hide their faces. It turned out that after the Libyan pipeline for weapons had been shut down, the IRA, or whatever variation on the theme this new faction went by, had been smuggling weapons from Estonia. The Russian FSB had already accused Estonia's volunteer defence force, the Kaitseliit, of supplying the guns, but when Caleb's cell had been exposed, they had all the proof they needed.'

'That's some serious shit,' says Lucas, with an incredulous look. 'Did you have any inkling that he was involved in that kind of stuff?'

'To be honest, not really,' I say, sighing deeply. 'Of course, in retrospect it should have been painfully obvious. Caleb never did do anything by halves, and it was a fitting homage to our mother. He loved her so deeply, but he was a prisoner to his own nature, essentially imposing self-exile on himself to avoid hurting those he loved most. What better way to honour a mother's love than to become a soldier for the cause that has always burned in her heart. He worshipped her from afar, a silent advocate toiling in the shadows. He had finally found something he could believe in, and he attacked it with the inherent vigour that was Caleb.'

'I wish I could tell you that was where it ended, but I can't. The day after Caleb's trial ended and he was sentenced to ten years in Mountjoy jail, I got a phone call from my father. It was three in the morning but I was lying awake in bed, staring at the ceiling. I hadn't slept in days, the stress of Caleb's trial and the effect it was having on my family kept me up most nights. I knew there was something wrong directly when I answered, my father whom I'd never seen shed a tear in his life was sobbing uncontrollably. I strained to grasp what he was saying but he was unintelligible, jabbering away like a madman. I hung up and jumped in the car, all the while trying desperately to get a handle on the panic that crawled out of every pore. When I arrived, the front door was open, and I could see all the way through the house to the backdoor swinging on its hinges. The scene that struck me as I stood in the kitchen and looked out at the back garden was oddly artificial. The blackness of the night was lit only by the porch light, casting an amber pool out into the shadows. The lighting and composition of the scene, the positioning of the players all had a surreal beauty to it like I was gazing at a living enactment of a Rembrandt or Caravaggio oil painting. The old rusted swing set of our childhood framed the stage and a ragged length of hosing dangled from the centre of the cross beam. Beneath it, my father held my mother in his arms, in a pose reminiscent of Michelangelo's Pietà, the grieving Virgin Mary cradling the lifeless body of Christ. The other end of the hose was still tight around my mother's neck, cutting deep into the flesh.'

Taking a deep drag on my smoke, I think back to that night. I don't know how long I stood there watching the scene from the doorway, it could have been seconds, minutes, hours. People came and went, some people talked to me, some people touched me, but I wasn't there. I was somewhere else entirely and the whole thing was a figment of my addled psyche, filling gaps in the narrative where omitted horrors left spaces. The mind is a tenuous thing but its capacity for self-preservation is formidable. At the first sign of assault the mind will dodge and feint, misdirect and manipulate, whatever fictions necessary to soften the blows.

'Man,' says Lucas, softly, shaking his head, 'I'm sorry.'

'Yeah, well,' I answer, trailing off into a few moments of contemplation. 'In those last few years she had lost her spark, you know? her drive. It pretty much took all of her will power just to get out of bed in the morning. But who's to say what was going on in her head when she decided to take her own life. No doubt, Caleb's incarceration was a catalyst in some way, the event that pushed her over the edge. Maybe it was the guilt of knowing it was the legacy of her own passion that brought him down in the end, or maybe it was simply the sorrow of having her loving son locked up in cage like an animal. Even though she hadn't seen him in years, she must have at least gained some solace in the thought that he was out in the world, experiencing life, living. I'm sure the not knowing gave some comfort, comfort that was torn from her when Caleb's fate was sealed. But it's impossible to say. She didn't leave a letter or communicate any reasoning for her actions. All she left was questions, questions I spent a long time asking myself, questions with no answers apart from the hollow echo of grief and guilt.'

'And what about Caleb?'

'I tried to visit him in jail but, as I expected, he refused to see me. You see, I know Caleb, sometimes I think I know him better than I know myself. Everyone is blind to aspects of themselves, the ego creating the fallacies that soothe men's minds, self-knowledge is hindered by self-preservation. But I could always see into the heart of Caleb, I could see the mechanisms that made him tick, and as sure as I know anything, I know he blamed me. I was the constant he clung to, I was the common element when the walls started the crumble, I was his point of focus when the ravages of his own mind sought to destroy him and I would be to blame for everything. Of that I have no doubt.'

The sky is beginning to bruise into evening as I sit on the bench, a sole spectator to the greatest show on earth. People hurry by on their way, squinting against the dusty winds that barrel through the park, lost in things gone by or things to come. I imagine I am the only person in the world experiencing this exact moment as it occurs and a sudden, unexpected sting of loneliness pierces my soul. The spring air is fresh and raw, and my eyes water. My hands are buried deep in my pockets and the collar of my overcoat is turned up, shielding me from the elements. Ripples trace their way across the surface of the pond and from somewhere unseen, a single quack of a duck is heard. A dull electric hum sees the park lamps ignite along the walkways and the bells fill the air, proclaiming the day is done.

I leave the park through Traitor's Gate, and make my way down Grafton Street, swaddled in the warmth of a pleasant melancholy. This is home after all, or was home when the word held meaning. The streets of Dublin have changed much since Joyce's flower bloomed, but his spirit is etched in the brickwork and flows in the gutters. No matter how you dress it up, the city has an old soul and rich poetry runs through her veins. The shops' shutters rattle closed and the caustic glare of enterprise fades to the heady glow of nightlife. I can almost feel the slowing of her pulse as she settles into the sultry rhythm. Street musicians busk out a living and their melodies carry through the cobbled side streets. A tinker boy with grubby hands and a cocky glint in his eye plays the tin whistle, while his young sidekick dances a jig. Further on, a girl strums a tune on her guitar, her eyes closed as she sings. Her voice is powerful yet soft, and her song is not for the onlookers, but for the world. She is a beauty, her cheeks flushed in the chill air, each breath of her passion visible for all to see. I stop to listen, and discreetly observe the small crowd that gathers. Each face is transfixed, drinking in her gift, each making it their own. When the small applause dies down, the tinkle of coins is heard in her guitar case, and for a moment I'm overcome by the beauty and simplicity of the exchange, its humanity.

The pungent aroma of malt and hops wafts from the pub doors as the revellers stream in, eager for the craic and the ceoil. I shake out a smoke and cup my hand around a dancing flame. Dragging deep, I push on into the night, anonymous. I am a child of the city, born and raised by her, nurtured and nourished, and as such I know the physicality of the city intimately. I know the feel of her contours and the play of light and shadow, and so I move through the crowds unnoticed, slipping through the natural gaps left between the living. I resonate at a frequency that doesn't alarm the innocents nor attract the vultures and therefore at some level I cease to exist. This is how I like it.

As we sat facing each other across the table, it occurred to me that something had changed in Uri, some imperceptible shift in his demeanour. It was an uncomfortable sensation, niggling at me like a tiny sliver of glass stuck in the sole of my foot. I could sense that something had changed, a subtle but fundamentally altering nuance. Was it Uri or was it my perception of Uri? Is there a difference? I felt like I had been staring at a painting for hours, trying to decipher an image in its manic strokes, only to realise it wasn't a painting but my own reflection in the remnants of a shattered mirror. Uri talked and I listened, but the words didn't make sense, just a stringing together of guttural sounds and whispers. I had felt ill, like the bile in my guts was bubbling and spitting and my stomach acid was corroding through its fleshy sack and scalding my insides. 'Jacob,' he had said, 'are you listening to me?' 'Yeah, sure I'm listening,' I had snapped back irritably, squirming around in my seat. My eyes darted around the room, distracted, twitchy. The room was a monument to clutter, not what you'd expect from a suave, manicured ponce like Uri. There were volumes upon volumes of books stacked on shelves that lined most of the walls. Meaty leather-bound tomes, gold embossed collections, tattered paperbacks, the stitching of their spines ragged and torn. Journals, periodicals, technical manuals, personal diaries, and in places the shelving had buckled under the weight of its burden. In the corners, more books were stacked in piles on the floor, a thick layer of dust visible on some of the jackets. From where I sat I could make out the names of some authors, classicists mixed with pulp purveyors, gods mingling with the nameless. There was apparently no adherence to any kind of order, as if the randomness of chaos had been purposely and painstakingly adhered to.

There were also other items stacked in corners and against shelves. There was an antique typewriter, missing the letters 'h' and 'f', sitting on the floor a few feet from me. There was one yellowed sheet of paper clamped in its jaws, the edges curled from the stuffy heat. A single line of script was visible, typed centre page. It read '*a conocerse a sí mismo es conocer la eternidad*'. Close to this, a viola with one string leaned nonchalantly against the wall, a white feather boa draped around its neck. In the centre of the room, an old telescope was affixed in a metal stand, a sequence of odd sized lenses clamped along a skeletal rod, like a spinal column stripped of its flesh. Crumpled star charts lay scattered on the floor at its feet, the absurdity of its existence compounded by the absence of any windows or skylight. An ornate bird cage hung slightly askew from a ceiling hook, and in it was perched a tiny bird whose downy feathers were an electric blue that I'm sure I've never seen before in nature, or anywhere for that fact. At the far end of the room, two steps led up to a doorway. The door was made of a dark, heavy wood with a deep red running through it and was wider and taller than an average door. The surface was cracked and scarred in a way that only the ravages of time can account for and its hinges were solid wrought iron clasps fashioned in a design reminiscent of a fleur-de-lis. I assumed it led out to a courtyard or a back alley as I could make out dust particles dancing in the crack of white light at the base of the door. By comparison to the general disarray of the space, the desk across from which Uri sat was completely bare, apart from a small antique clock that ticked incessantly during our meetings. Constructed from what looked like brass, it was a square case resting on four ball feet with a burnished circular dial and a single hour hand. The gears and cogwheels of the workings were visible through an intricately crafted copper mesh and a small silver bell hung at its centre. After all the times I'd sat in that chair and listened as my fate unravelled before me, there was always something about that clock that didn't seem right to me. It only struck me in that moment how curious it was that the clock was facing me and not Uri.

Winding down toward College Green, I pause for a moment outside the gates of Trinity College and peer through the black iron railings. Beneath the grey, floodlit columns of learning, students gather for the night's festivities, fresh faces flushed with the eager rush of youth and independence. They own the night and all it has to offer, and so I leave them to their lives and continue on down Dame Street. The traffic runs bumper to bumper and the frustration is palpable, horns honking, nerves frayed. Rumbling engines cough soot onto grey pillars and the noxious fumes burn my sinuses. I weave my way through to the other side and duck down Crow Street towards Temple Bar. The cobble streets are buzzing with activity, locals and tourists feeding off each other to the beat of the bodhrán and the whine of the uillean pipe. Porter by the pint and culture by the coin is the name of the game, and the narrow streets teem with willing players as the black cloak of night settles. Old brickwork is splashed with vibrant colours and warmly lit by muted lanterns while the pubs and restaurants peddle their wares.

When I was young, the side streets and alleyways were darker, mystery and wonder to be found around every corner, the very air suffused with bohemian spirit. Caleb and I would spend hours rooting through the second-hand clothes stores, the musty smell of mothballs and incense, looking to score that vintage gold mine. We would spend Saturday afternoons in the many record shops, flicking through old vinyl in search of rarities or bargains. In the summer months, artisan jewellers would throw a blanket on the pavement and display their merchandise, bracelets, broaches, necklaces, all lovingly hand-crafted pieces of artistry. An old man would stand on his corner every day and recite poetry with his soft-cap clenched in his hand. Even though his shoes were broken and his clothes were dirty and ragged, there was an unyielding pride in his manner, an unbreakable core to his being. His white beard was yellowing around his mouth and dark bags hung under his eyes, but he would hold his chin up high, stoic, a man in full. Long gone are those hazy summer days when we believed we were the first to truly fall in love, the first to comprehend the essence of art and music, the first to commune with spirituality and the universe. I chuckle to myself at the maudlin nature of my thoughts, and move on through the crowd, climbing the steps up to the Ha'penny Bridge that crosses the River Liffey. There's still time.

Across town a young man strides confidently down the street, a spring in his step and a song in his heart. He's well dressed in a trim navy overcoat, pinstripe shirt and neatly pressed slacks, and on his hands he wears soft leather gloves. He exudes an air of quiet sophistication and the confidence of a man who has achieved a certain measure of success in his life. A gust of wind momentarily blows a lock of hair into his eyes and he carefully smoothes it back into place. A young mother walks by pushing her baby in a pram and blushes ever so slightly as the handsome gentleman favours her with a debonair smile. As he passes, her mind wanders innocently to a life she might have had if things had have been different for her, but the thought is nothing but a fleeting fancy, and so she continues on her way. Anyway, she thinks, as the gentleman disappears around the corner, there's obviously some lucky young thing waiting for him tonight.

'You seem distracted today, Jacob,' he had said, leaning across the table and patting my forearm. I was instantly repulsed by his touch, those stumpy, bloated sausage fingers and those gaudy rings, each one probably worth a small fortune, giving his hand an unnatural weight. I pulled away and leaned back in the chair, folding my arms across my chest. I was feeling nauseous and the uncomfortable itch of paranoia was putting me in a petulant frame of mind.

'Yeah, well,' I said, 'it feels like I've been your lackey for a long time now and have fucking nothing to show for it.' My tone of voice had surprised me. I was usually so rattled by Uri's presence that I generally didn't say much, just murmuring in acquiescence or, when I did ask a question, stumbling over my words like an idiot. I felt like a whipped dog, daring to beg for scraps at his master's table. But I was reaching the end of my tether, in body, mind and spirit, and this decline had brought about a sense of abandon in me. It was time to finish what I had started and I was done playing puppet. One of Uri's black caterpillar eyebrows was raised in an expression of mild amusement, but he sat silently and let me go on. 'I've held up my end of the bargain, haven't I?' I continued, a little giddy now, feeling my heartbeat pound unevenly in my chest. 'I did whatever you asked of me, even though each fucking time I lost a little piece of myself, died a little every time.' My voice was getting gradually louder, and it felt as if I was a spectator in the room, listening to myself, unable to change what was happening. 'How many times have I done your bidding? How long do I have to spend in this shithole before you decide I'm done?' I was standing now, gesturing wildly. Was I sobbing now or was I just shaking in anger, I couldn't tell, but from a great distance I could feel my body wracking with spasms. 'How many more times does it have to be before you give me what you promised me?' I shouted, coming to a climax of grief and rage. 'You've taken everything from me, now for Christ's sake, GIVE ME CALEB!'

The last words hung in the air between us for an eternity, and then a thin silence crawled in to take their place. I flopped back down into the chair, drained, deflated, spent. I looked at Uri and he me. There was the hint of a smile on his lips and he nodded his head slowly back and forth. After a while and without a word, he pushed his chair back and got to his feet. Turning his back to me, he began fingering though the spines of the books piled on the shelf closest to him, searching for something in particular. Apparently finding what he was looking for, he pulled a small book from where it stood, wedged between a thick medical encyclopaedia and an autobiography of a man called Theodor Feigl, and took a seat once more. Slowly and almost tenderly, he placed the book face up on the table and gently pushed it across so that it sat right in front of me. The title of the book was 'The Cerulean Dream' by Emmanuel Cortez. Leaning forward in his seat, Uri fixed me with an enigmatic look, and spoke softly but with purpose.

'All you need to know can be found within these pages.' He paused for a heartbeat, and somewhere inside me I knew what he was about to say next.

'This is the last time, Jacob,' he said, the rush and thunder of my own blood pumping in my ears, 'You're going home'.

Crossing the bridge, the acrid brine of the Liffey is carried on the wind and, left and right, the city spreads out before me. I pass a beggar with one or two rotten teeth left in his head and his trousers pegged off where his legs used to be. His skin bears the scabs and wounds of the user, the stigmata of the unwell, and he proffers a plastic mug for offerings and a sign that declares he is indeed both homeless and hungry. So disconnected from the bustle of others, I recoil slightly in surprise when he addresses me directly, but he speaks in a tongue I'm not familiar with. He repeats himself over and over, an urgent mantra, his frustration carved in deep furrows across his brow and cheeks. Just for an instant, I think I understand the words coming from his mouth, like the echo of a nursery rhyme from before memory. But each time my mind strains I feel the loss of purchase, as if climbing a staircase made from quicksand, inevitably succumbing to the tiresome weight of effort. I surrender a shrug of apology and drop a note in his cup. He responds with a high whiny cackle, completely void of humour, and starts to clap his hands and jiggle about as if dancing to a jolly tune only he can hear. The performance is disturbing, the stumps of his lost limbs waving around, but no one notices, and this disturbs me most of all.

I make my way down the quays, the hollowness of his cackle stalking me, nesting and laying spider eggs in my head. The steal clamp tightens on my mind and my body responds with an icy shiver. I can feel the jangle of my frayed nerve endings and a burning sensation behind my eyes. I need to stop off for the cure, so I turn down into Spinster's Way. The narrow laneway is ripe with the toxic stench of puddled urine and dumpsters overflowing with rotting garbage. Extractor fans belch out a hot mist of stale grease from the back entrances of burger bars and fried chicken franchises. I duck in under the low doorway of the Spinster Inn, grateful for the waft of booze and cigarette smoke that greets me.

The gentleman whistles as he walks, brimming with the excitement that only anticipation can bring. He was looking forward to seeing her, looking forward to kissing her lips and holding her tight. He felt like he knew her heart and soul and that this was definitely the one. He knew it was a little silly and old-fashioned to think in that way, what with everyone being so cynical these days, but it wasn't naïve to believe in true love, was it? No, no it wasn't, he thinks, smiling to himself, I'm just a romantic is all. His brows knit together momentarily as he feels about in his coat for the present he brought for her, but his expression clears as he pulls it from his inside pocket. The piece is a precious stone of a light azure blue, set in a silver clasp and hangs from a fine silver chain. He holds it up to admire it, allowing himself a moment of kudos for his eye for things of beauty. Yes, he thought, what woman would not love such a thing. Securing it in his pocket once more, he continues on towards his rendezvous, quietly confidant that tonight all his expectations will be realised.

I climb the stairs to the lounge area on the second floor, the stairs creaking under my weight as I go. The walls of the narrow staircase are scarred with the insights and musing of young poets and philosophers. 'Yur ma sucks cock,' reveals one diligent scribe. 'Maggie B takes it up the arse for scag,' suggests another. The city heaves with drinking spots and watering holes but I prefer to remain unnoticed, so I pick a place that serves my purpose. A loose strand of memory steered me here, a bar whose patronage cower in the half-light, counting the beats until they are forgotten or forget themselves. The décor of the lounge is a drab affair with a few booths and tables placed indiscriminately around the room. In its infancy, the carpet looks like it had a recurring bold pattern in reds and yellows, but years of spilt booze and ash, fag burns and old gum had worn it down to a shit brown. Likewise, the wallpaper had a satin sheen to it with a raised velvet motif running floor to ceiling, but the smoke of a thousand lives had choked its colour to a piss stained yellow. The few drinkers that murmur between themselves throw furtive glances in my direction but they clock me as a fellow broken brother and go back to their drinks. The old bartender gives me a small nod but, apart from that, maintains a statuesque pose of lethargic suspicion with a dash of contempt for good measure. It looks like the well practiced expression of professional detachment which decrees, 'I'll serve you what you want, but step out of line and there'll be trouble.'

He's old as the hills, this fella, his skin loose and drooping from his body as if he's in the very slow process of melting. His eyes hang bloodshot and a little milky but I can tell from his look that there's definitely some fire left in the old boy, a hint of the troublemaker he was in another lifetime. A few wisps of white hair are drawn across his pate and mottled liver spots spatter his skull. The sleeves of his white shirt are rolled to the elbow revealing the faded splodge of an old tattoo on his forearm, a dagger through a heart with the scroll of an old flame's name across the centre. Her identity has long since been claimed by the wrinkling and sagging of time and, in a brief moment of curiosity, I wonder who she was.

I get a pint and a double whisky, served to me in silence, and then he saunters to the other end of the bar to leave me to my drinking. Sparking up a Johnny Blue, I inhale the first drag deep in to my lungs and hold it there until I feel that first dizzying rush to the head and then release a plume of smoke with a satisfied sigh. A couple of gulps and the pint is three-quarters done, with the whisky that follows it adding quite a valid point to the discussion. The thirst is on me something fierce as it tends to be when there's work to be done, and so I motion to the squire for another round as a precursor to many more. Every now and then someone wanders to the bar to fill their cup, but I pay them no heed and in turn they leave me be. That's how it is with those who want to be forgotten, it's a process of removal from the human race, until in the end you're unrecognisable to anyone. When that finality is reached, only then can you truly forget yourself since there is no-one left to remind you of who you are. I know a little something about that.

I find myself thinking back to Sarah and Lily's funeral. In the memory I see myself from outside of my own body, as if I am an observer, dislocated, but this is how memories come to me these days. It feels as if my mind will only allow these recollections by distancing myself from the pain I felt, numbing me to a hurt that would surely eat at me until there was nothing left. And so I see myself, standing by the graveside, black suit, black tie, black shoes, black. The other people who attended have all gone home, I wanted to be alone. I wanted to be alone with Sarah. With Lily. After that day, I removed myself from the living world. Family, friends, colleagues, I pushed them away until they stopped pushing back. I deconstructed the life I had had, a life which had ceased to exist for me now that Sarah and Lily were gone. Bit by bit, I simply removed all the bonds and moorings that bind a man to the life he lives, and left myself to float adrift. Only then could I truly lose myself. I'll never be that man again. I couldn't even if I tried. He doesn't exist anymore.

I enjoy a good stroll in the cool night air, the gentleman muses to himself, a whimsical smile playing on his lips. It gets the heart pumping and the blood flowing and a man can feel alive on a night like this. His mind drifts as he walks, thoughts about how their life would be together from here on in, when they finally stop the pretence, the games, and profess their undying love for each other. She won't let me down, he assures himself, not this girl. He feels in his coat pocket just to make sure the gift is safe and sound, and the smooth, cool feel of it against his palm soothes him and renews his confidence. She had looked so pretty with that necklace on, he remembers, even when the disease had all but claimed her, when her body had been covered in pustules and sores. Even with the crushing disfigurement of the illness she still maintained this ethereal beauty, this incorruptible inner light. The was no question that he would take care of her himself, he wasn't going to abandon her in one of those sick homes, where the nurses leave you to wallow in your own filth because they're too busy flirting with the doctors. Gold digging whores, he thinks, a flash of white anger causing the muscles in his jaw to tense and flex ever so slightly. Anyway, what else would I do for the woman who single-handedly raised me, fed me, clothed me, after the rummy masquerading as my father took a walk? We were better off without him anyways. No more lying awake at night, staring into the darkness, feeling guilty that you hope he goes into her room and not yours when you hear his key finally slide into the lock. No, this is what you do for the people you love and the people who love you back, devotion without pause. His mind drifts back to the daily ritual of caring for her, when she was too weak to hold a spoon or use the bathroom by herself. Her skin had become paper thin, almost translucent, and was drawn taut over every bone in her frail body. Every vertebrae of her spine was visible when she was hunched over in pain, the hacking coughs sending spasms of agony through her core. Her once auburn hair had turned grey and lifeless, and towards the end he remembers discreetly collecting the clumps of hair that were left on her pillow, because the loss of her hair, of all things, made her cry.

Each time he would carry her into the bathroom to bathe her he would marvel at her weightlessness, as if her body was constructed with the hollow bones of a baby bird. No matter how hot he ran her bath water, she would always shiver the entire time and stare straight ahead into nothingness, perhaps seeking refuge from the pain and humiliation in some hidden corner of her mind. He had very little time left for himself, of course, what with work and the constant care and supervision of his mother, but this didn't bother him, this was the truest expression of love. He remembers those fleeting moments of reprieve from her suffering, those few minutes between administering the last injection of the day and when it sent her off to a dreamless sleep. He would sit by her bedside and stroke her forehead as she drifted in and out of consciousness, hating himself for the flicker of repulsion he felt at the touch of her cold, clammy skin. Just as she would float away she would look up at him, her eyes already half lost in the fog and whisper, 'Nobody will ever love you like I do.'

I come out of the Spinster and turn the corner onto O'Connell Street. I feel the flush of the drink on my cheeks and the heat in my belly on this cold night. This street is like any other city main street, any vestige of culture and taste having been raped and strangled by the hyperactive appetites of modern society. Quick fix junkies and junk food drunks stagger around under the non-stop kaleidoscope of cheap indulgence. The music of sirens fill the air, a constant reminder that such ugliness comes at a price paid out in pounds of flesh. Shifty-eyed dealers congregate at the statue's feet, twitching and shrugging while O'Connell himself stands on high, surrounded by dogs and angels. I weave through the clatter and yell and pass under the columns of the General Post Office where Pearce and the boys made their stand on that faithful day in 1916. I can still see the bullet holes in the concrete under the frantic flicker of lights from a nearby amusement arcade. I walk on by, the excited screams and candy cries, the game glare and the bumper burn, all tumble out of noisy doors and shatter on the cold pavement. I beat a path across to the other side and duck for cover down Cathedral Street, the deep clang of the bells of St.Mary's offering the promise of refuge against the madness of the night. The Pro-cathedral looms high and formidable against its inky backdrop and worshippers and stragglers climb the steps to take in a late mass. I slip in amongst them and pass through the archway into divine sanctuary.

Inside the great chamber the service has already begun, so I move quietly up the side aisle, shielded somewhat by the huge granite pillars that support the high dome ceiling. There is an odd incongruity to the architecture of the interior, with both Roman and Greek influences juxtaposed in a battle for aesthetic dominance. The warm scent of burning candle wax and the heady aroma of incense wafts by as I progress slowly along the pews. The marble floor offers no traction, and I experience a pleasant feeling of gliding, as if yielding to some unseen force. Attendance is sparse, barely registering in this huge tomb, so I stop about half way up the church and sidle in to take a seat away from the other congregants. The altar is an impressive affair, a beautifully sculpted inlay of two angels supplicating before God, and an expansive stained glass window of the Blessed Virgin Mary provides a backdrop to this spiritual stage. A young priest stands front and centre, his arms out-stretched as he speaks as if beseeching his flock, pleading them to accept God's love into their hearts. He strikes me as almost inappropriately young, with his smooth boyish features and hair parted to the side, but his manner exudes the confidence and self-assurance of a much older man. There is a pleasant timbre to his voice, an almost melodic lilt to his words, and I find myself comforted by them as I sit here. My head swims agreeably with the lock of drink and I allow myself to drift a little as I listen to his words, unburdened for a moment, set free from the hardships of living. A choir of white-robed young boys breaks into angelic song, offering up devout petition to the Lord. The sound fills the church, the acoustics full and powerful, and I surprise myself by how moved I am by it all.

Amidst the sound there is a faint ticking, subtle at first but then as I become more aware of it, it becomes the only sound I hear. Its insistence drags me back from where my thoughts roamed and I strain to identify the origin of this intrusion. I scan the church, searching for someone or something causing this ticking but it comes from close by, as if I held my watch close to my ear. I look to my left and my heart lurches in my chest as I realise there is an old man sitting not two feet away from me in the same pew. My mind churns and reels, paranoia and discomfort burrowing in the soft tissue of my brain stem. How is it possible I didn't see him come in? Have I been sleeping? Could it be that I'm still asleep? The last thought sends an uneasy current through my body and I can feel the skin tighten on the back of my neck and behind my balls. The old man pays me no attention even though I stare. He kneels down on the hard wood and fingers black rosary beads while he whispers an endless prayer. There is not a trace of hair left on his head and his eyebrows are wild, unkempt bushes of grey. He has the large ears and long nose of a man of years, and his bony frame looks all the more skinny in a slightly over-sized black suit. From where I sit I can make out a thin layer of dust on the shoulders and sleeves of his jacket. As his frail fingers pass from one bead to the next, the process seems to pain him, and a visible tremor causes his whole body to quiver giving the unsettling illusion that he is somehow out of focus, there, but somewhere else also. From his long nose, drops of blood fall to the marble floor. Tick. Tick. Tick. Each droplet splashes onto the cold, white marble, his blood a dark crimson, congealed and viscous, yet he continues with his prayers as if unaware. The choir boys have stopped singing and the young priest is reciting a passage from the bible.

'...*I saw heaven opened, and behold, a white horse. And He who sat on him was called Faithful and True, and in righteousness He judges and makes war...*' Tick. Tick. Tick. I try to get the old man's attention but he's lost in his prayers. I have an uncomfortable feeling in my chest, and a sense of panic and dread slowly spiral up inside me, the pulse of my heart beat in my ears muffling all other sounds. I try again, slightly louder this time, discretion sacrificed on the altar of anxiety. But again, nothing. It feels as if I'm trying to call out in a high wind and the words have been snapped from my mouth and flung to the farthest corners of the earth.

'...*His eyes were like a flame of fire, and on His head were many crowns. He had a name written that no one knew except Himself. He was clothed in a robe dipped in blood, and His name is called The Word of God...*' Tick. Tick. Tick. I shuffle up beside him and reach out to him, trying to lightly touch his shoulder without startling him, but still no response. I squeeze his shoulder gently and whisper to him but he continues with his liturgy, eyes cast down to the floor, his lips moving soundlessly. I feel like whatever thin strands are keeping me from loosing my mind altogether are unravelling and I'm lifting off the ground, condemned to the abyss of insanity for all time. The panic screams and claws at me from the inside, finding new and unexplored heights of horror, and the din in my ears is so painful, I think I feel a trickle of blood run down the side of my cheek. I grab him by both shoulders and shake him violently, screaming at him to listen to me, pleading with him. And just like that, he looks me in the eyes and the world is plunged into complete silence once more. His eyes are a dusty, powder blue and full of kindness and love. He looks at my face, looks at the sweat running down my brow, looks at my mouth twisted and frozen, a string of spittle hanging between my lips. He slowly brings his left hand up to his face and, putting a long, slender finger to his lips, emits a long hushing noise. His face is mere inches from my own and there is something almost intimate in the way he looks at me. Taking his finger from his lips he points towards the altar, and in a gravelly voice that crackles up from deep inside him, he whispers to me, pausing between each word. 'You're. Not. Listening.'

'*...Now out of His mouth goes a sharp sword, that with it He should strike the nations. And He Himself will rule them with a rod of iron. He Himself treads the winepress of the fierceness and wrath of Almighty God.*'

The handsome young man stands in a doorway, sheltering himself from the downpour. It won't last, he thinks to himself as he smoothes back his hair, I'll just wait it out. He looks at the people scurrying to and fro, hoods pulled tight, newspapers held overhead. A young lady bundles past, one hand holding her skirts in place while the other struggles with a thin umbrella, its spokes already bent and mangled from the gusts of wind and rain. Her hair is soaked and lank locks are strewn across her face. There is something about the girl, perhaps the angle of her jaw line or the slope of her brow, which makes him think of Anthousa. Ah, Anthousa. Her name came from the Greek word for flower, and that was what she was, possessing of a natural beauty and delicacy that swept him away. But she wasn't the one, he admits to himself, a shadow crossing his features as he thinks back to the night she broke his heart.

It was a night just like this one, and it was to be the night that he professed his love by bestowing on her the gift that was closest to his heart and said all the things he felt, but found hard to put into words. As like tonight, he had made the extra effort with his appearance, sporting a beautifully tailored new suit and shoes of a soft Italian leather. He had worn the cologne that he knew she liked, dabbing it sparingly onto his freshly shaven jaw, aware that a lady likes a man's scent to be subtle and discreet. His hair had been newly cut and slicked back neatly with an aromatic wax. He had also bought flowers, a small arrangement of red lilies that he felt captivated her essence. On the night in question he had rounded the corner to see her chatting with some of her girl friends so he held back and waited, knowing that she would appreciate the fact that he hadn't intruded. Also, this was their night and he didn't want to share a single moment of it with anyone else. How selfish of me, he had thought to himself with a small smile, but love was a greedy beast that would not be done until it was sated, and he was at its mercy. After a while, she had broken away from her friends and made her way slowly down the street, the click of her heels calling to him. His heart went out to her as she rubbed her arms for warmth, the night had obviously had turned colder than she had dressed for, but soon she would be wrapped in his warm embrace.

As she turned down a narrow alley way, he had crossed over to surprise her, attempting a lightness of foot to achieve his goal. And it had succeeded, giving her a momentary start as he emerged from the shadows behind her, her hand going to her chest as she caught her breath. 'Jesus, you scared the shit outta me,' she had said, reprimanding him with those big blue eyes. 'Anthousa,' he had said, saying her name as if for the first time, feeling out each vowel and consonant, tasting each one individually. 'Sure, whatever you want,' she had said, eyeing him from head to toe. 'The flowers are a bit much, buddy, you get what you pay for,' she added, a half smile on her full red lips. A trace of confusion crossed his features but disappeared just as quickly, his fingers tracing the smooth surface of the necklace in his coat pocket. Taking it in his hand he moved toward her. 'I brought you a present, Anthousa, it's something that's very important to me and I feel that you should be the one to wear it, my love.' She had backed away every so slightly, looking over his shoulder and then over hers. 'Listen mister,' she had said, a strange look on her face, 'role-playing is fine with me, but first let's get business outta the way.' No response. 'Eh, hello?' she continued, scorn tainting her tone, 'anybody home in there? If you wanna fuck you gotta produce the bleedin' dosh, right?' The furrows returned to his brow as he struggled to understand the words coming from her mouth. 'Anthousa,' he said, dropping the flowers in a puddle of dirty drain water and taking her by the arm, 'why are you being like this when I'm trying to tell you how much I love you?' His grip tightened on her. 'Okay, mister,' she said, her demeanour different now, fear visible in her eyes as they searched his. 'Just let me go, right? I won't cause any trouble. Let's just pretend this never happened, okay?' He let the necklace drop to the pavement as he took hold of her other arm, his frame shaking with anger, his eyes dark pools of confusion and rage. 'Did I mean nothing to you?' he asked through gritted teeth, bringing his face close to hers, 'were you just stringing me along the whole time?' 'Listen, mister,' she said in a small, quivering voice, 'I do love you, yeah? I'll even give yeh a freebie, okay? Just please let me go, you're hurting me.' 'I'm hurting you?' he spat back incredulously, 'I'm hurting you? I give you everything and all I ask in return is for you to love me and this is how you treat me?' His hands moved to her neck as he tried to stifle the lies that spewed from her. The tears rolled down his cheeks as he tightened his hold around her throat. She turned out to be just like all the others, lying whores who took his love for granted and played him for a fool. Her breath came in strangled wheezes and her big, blue eyes bulged in terror as she used her last strength to claw and scrab at his face. But his grip was too strong. He could feel her windpipe give in to his crushing effort, a small deflation beneath his thumbs as the life ran out of her. He released his hold on her, letting her body crumble unceremoniously to the ground. He looked down at her in disgust and then his expression switched to concern as he scanned the gutters for the necklace. After a few frantic moments of pawing around in the muddy detritus, he exhaled in relief, fishing out the necklace by its thin chain. Using the corner of his shirt he polished the sky-blue stone, making sure to remove any trace of dirt from the smaller details of the silver clasp. Depositing it in his coat pocket, he walked away down the alley, never pausing once to look back.

Standing in the doorway he traces his forefinger over the surface of the necklace. Tonight will be different, he reassures himself, tonight will be the first night of the rest of my life, a life of happiness with beautiful Theodosia. As the last drops of rain disappear from the sky, the handsome gentleman makes his way out into the night, a spring in his step and a song in his heart.

I stagger down side streets and around corners, the rain now heavy and wet, blurring my vision. Splashing through dark puddles, the damp air is infused with the noxious odour of the sewers, clogging my nose and throat with the struggle of panicked breath. I need to get out into the open but, the city, she holds me under with an iron grip, throwing up wall after wall as I search blindly for escape. She turns all her attention to me, the weight of her stare all but tearing me apart and scattering me on the winds. Who are you? she asks, her voice hollow and ancient. I cry out an answer but it doesn't do. Who are you? she asks again, this time her voice is the small, innocent cadence of a little girl and comes from inside my head. What do you want from me? I scream back at her. But just as I knew it was she who talked to me, I now knew she was gone, leaving me alone in this dark alley, searching the sliver of heaven visible between the rooftops for answers to questions I didn't know.

I'm spat out into oncoming traffic, their horns screaming in protest as I stumble across the sea of lights and metal. Nameless faces scowl at me through narrow eyes and bubbled windscreens, baring their teeth at me in white knuckle fury. The lives of others do not concern me right now, what concerns me is the search for air, to be resuscitated before I perish, and so I scale the iron railings of the Garden of Remembrance and drop down into its shaded solitude.

The garden is a sunken cruciform and I make my way down to take refuge in one of its arms, the noise and madness of the streets already falling away into the distance. The high walls of the cross shield me from the outside world and I feel the terror inside me slowly abate. The rain responds in kind with empathy, fading to a light drizzle that plants cool butterfly kisses on my cheeks and forehead. A shallow pool runs the length of the crucifix and my eye is momentarily drawn to the swords and spears of free Irishmen cast in mosaic on the water floor. Taking a seat on a bench in the right arm, I lean my head back, eyes closed, immersing myself in the calm. I drink down the fresh night, drawing it deep into me, revitalised, resurrected.

After a spell, my eyes open onto a new world, lush and green, crisp and vital. Shaking a smoke loose from a damp pack, it takes a few tries to light but finally gives in to its fate. The iron statue of the Children of Lir rises up before me stirring memories from my childhood, its twisted metal depicting the moment of transformation when the children were turned into swans. Our mother used to regale us with such bedtime stories when the fire still burned inside her, and the worlds they created in our heads fuelled our young imaginations. The story goes, that Lir was displeased when Bodb Dearg was made king of the Tuatha Dé Danann and so to appease him, Bodb gave his daughter, Aoibh, to Lir to make his wife. Together they had four children, Fionnuala, Aodh and twins, Conn and Fiachra. However, Aoibh died and Bodb sent yet another daughter, Aoife, to be Lir's new wife. Aoife was consumed by jealousy for the love the children had for each other and for Lir. She conspired to have the children killed but when her servants refused to do her bidding, she tried herself, only to lack the courage to follow through. Instead she used her magick to transform the children into swans. On realising what had happened, Bodb retaliated by turning Aoife into an air demon for all eternity. In their swan form, the children were condemned to spend three hundred years on Lough Derravaragh, three hundred years in the Sea of Moyle and three hundred years on the Isle of Glora, upon which time the spell could only be broken by a priest's blessing. After nine hundred years of suffering, the sound of church bells beckoned them to land where a priest finally freed them from their curse. Returned to human form, their ancient bodies soon died and they were reunited with their loving parents in heaven. I remember myself and Caleb as young boys, feasting on this tale of old. We interpreted the story differently then, viewing the transformation into swans as a gift rather than a curse. To be set free from your human form, given the ability to fly, to assume the powerful grace of the swan and even more, to live for hundreds of years. The prospect of such a thing made us giddy with possibility. Now, as I sit here looking up at the statue, watching flesh become feather, I find myself for the first time understanding it for the curse it really was.

Crushing the butt of my cigarette underfoot, I pull myself to my feet with a weary sigh. There's work to be done before this night is through and time, they say, waits for no man.

It happens like it has happened many times before. The dream is real and reality shifts and warps, bending to the will of subconscious desires. As I move through the streets I feel like I'm descending a long staircase into a state of lucid dreaming, where actions and the pulse that drives them have been pre-determined by a secret voice deep inside me. I relinquish control of my mind and body to that which I don't fully understand but trust implicitly, secure in the knowledge that a dream is in fact only a dream. In truth I am at peace, content to surrender myself to a few heartbeats that defy definition, compartmentalisation, comprehension. It is a freedom that I have seldom found of late and I welcome it, like I will welcome death when the time comes.

Turning corner after corner, the ebb of foot traffic heralds the black hole of urbanity. High-rise flats tower unsteadily in the black sky, a baby cries out, a dog howls, somewhere a bottle is smashed, but desolation is the loudest sound tonight. There is a beauty to it though, as there is a beauty to all things if the angle of perception is true, and as I walk down the side streets, my heart is full. Across the street, two girls huddle together lighting a smoke, a tall bleach blond with hunched shoulders and a petite brunette with a lavish mane of brown curls. Their short skirts and exposed legs offer little defence against the chill air, so they stamp from foot to foot to warm their blood. They pause in their parlance when a car drives slowly by, flicking open their coats in exhibition, but the faceless figure drives on into the night. After a few minutes have passed the girls hug each other and move off in opposite direction in search of better corners on better streets.

I stand still against a doorway and watch the small girl as she clicks along the pavement in and out of flickering pools of light. And then I see him. A slight disturbance in the shadows of an alleyway as she passes by, a slight ripple in the dark corners. I make my way across the street, purpose in my stride, the rush of blood making my nerves tingle as my heart thumps on in my chest, while at the same time an ethereal calm envelops me. I reach the mouth of the alley just as he emerges from the darkness and he stops dead, his expression battling with a scuffle of conflicting emotions, but as always there is only one inevitable victor in the fight, and that is fear.

'What do you want from me?' he asks, nervously running a palm back through his hair, 'who are you?' These are not questions that concern me. Nothing of what is said concerns me, just sounds and shapes strung together and bleated out into the air between us. He already knows the answers to all the questions he asks and so I wait, passively watching the dawn of understanding in his eyes. The moment is beautiful, peaceful, and I am overcome with a sense of blissful contentment that wells up from within me. Moving in close now, I can see tears in his eyes, the same tears he cried when he was brought into this world, the same tears he wept as a boy and the same tears he shed as a man. And just for that moment he encompasses all three, and for the first time in his life he is whole. He stands motionless as I lean in, bringing my lips close to his ear. There is now nothing between us, I am him and he is me. A single word is formed on my lips, a word I do not know but speak nonetheless. The word is simple yet complex, it is the part and also the whole. It is a word that can only be heard once and then no more. I whisper softly to him and, for a fraction of eternity, the world is his. And then he is gone. The lifeless shell that contained him falls to the ground and once more the shadows swallow him up.

It's been a long time since I've stood here in the driveway looking up at the house that was my childhood home. Although I've also known it as an adult, its character, the essence of its homeliness, is a spectre from my youth and as such the house seems small, dwarfed by age. Its dimensions seem stunted, its colours faded. This is a stop I have forced myself to make, the estrangement between me and my father being painful and seared with guilt. A man who lost his wife, who lost one son and whose other son pushed him away by degrees before clinically removing himself from his life in an attempt to lose himself. It's no surprise then that reluctance keeps me out here in the drizzle with dribbles of rain running down my face.

I'm tired from the nights toil, drained of energy and grated from the instability that teases my frazzled mind and standing here amidst the ghosts of my childhood only adds to the surreal state of things. The neighbourhood was always quiet and still is, a lot of the houses now serving as the last resting place for the aged. Most homes are dimly lit with evening warmth but my father's house is cloaked in darkness. The crunch of the gravel beneath my feet is the only sound to be heard as I walk around the side of the house. Bending down to turn up the corner of the welcome mat by the side door, I'm mildly amused to see a key still lying where it's always been. On entering, I turn on a small hall light and speak my father's name, but no answer comes. I move from room to room, memories entangled in the web of gloom that suffocates every nook and cranny. The house is cold. Cold and damp. There is a heavy musty smell hanging in the air and it's tinged with the faint stench of rot. I feel a sadness come over me, like I am the last man on earth and I'm condemned to walk for all time through the debris and rubble of what once was humanity.

Hesitantly, I push open the door to my father's study and already I feel something I've felt once before, an awareness that someone is there with me in the room, ensconced in the darkness.

'Who's there?' comes a low growl from the far corner of the room. 'Make yourself known.'

'It's me, Da,' I reply, the words catching in my throat. 'I've come to see how you are,' I say, finding my feet and following his voice across the room.

'Is that you, son,' he asks, his tone guarded and suspicious but less aggressive than before.

'Yeah, it's me. I thought I'd pay you a visit while I'm home for a couple of days. Why are you sitting here in the pitch dark?'

Reaching out, I flick the switch on an old, green table lamp that has sat on my father's writing desk for as long as I can remember. The light finds my father sitting in his armchair and for a split second I feel a cry in my chest as the shock deals me a powerful blow. He has aged dramatically, his once brown locks have turned to a dirty grey and hang greasy and matted against his forehead. He has let his beard grow out and it has the wild, unkempt look of a man struggling to maintain his sanity. He wears a raggedy, navy jumper that hasn't seen a wash for a long time, stains and encrusted food spattered down its front. But all this pales in comparison to the alarm I feel on seeing his eyes. Any colour they once had has been replaced by a sick, waxy film and thin, spidery capillaries are clustered near his tear ducts. I am stunned into silence at the sight of him and minutes pass as I take a seat across from him.

'Sure why would a blind man need the lights on,' he says, as if there had been no pause in our conversation. He cackles in a way that makes me very uneasy and reaches for a bottle of Glenfiddich from the sideboard. There's a few fingers left in the bottle and from the look of him he's seen it all the way through. His movements are jerky and his mouth moves constantly, even when silent, as if searching for an expression but never finding it.

'When did it happen?' I ask concerned, leaning over and putting a hand on his forearm.

'Ah, who knows,' he mutters, shrugging off my hand and groping around on the sideboard for an empty glass. 'I'm sure you'll join your auld fella in a drink since you've bothered to come all this way, eh?' he asks with thinly veiled bitterness that I can see from his face he regrets immediately. I swig down a glass to calm my nerves and pour myself another, which elicits a knowing chuckle from my father.

'The apple doesn't fall very far from the tree, does it, son?'

As we sit here across from each other, all the things that should be said flick through my mind but I have no idea where to begin and, if I'm honest with myself, I have no desire to either. These unsaid things sit heavy on us in this dark study, burdens that cripple our souls and warp our features. Time goes by in silence, not an uncomfortable silence, we know each other too well, but a weary silence. As the heat of the malt whisky emanates through my body, a question that I have asked myself one too many times in the recent past drifts lazily into my thoughts. How did I get to this place? The answer eludes me, the journey obscured.

'You should have seen her back then, the first time I met her,' says my father, talking to himself as much as me, his voice clouded with drink and reminiscence. 'I was sitting in the Twisted Stair, sipping on a coffee and reading an old Flann O'Brien novel, minding my own business. I saw her walk in and go to the counter to order, of course everybody saw her. That was the thing with your mother, she turned heads. When she walked into a room she lit it up. She was so beautiful.' There's a slur in his voice and I can hear the restraint of the tears being held back. 'I was more surprised than anyone when she walked across the café toward me and took a seat, her wild shock of red curls pinned back with a silver clasp. And that was the moment I fell in love with her. You don't believe in that kind of thing until it happens to you, but I loved her from the first time I laid eyes on her.'

Although I was close to my father growing up, I'd never heard him talk like this. He was always a kind and gentle man but definitely not one given to verbalising his emotions, so I listen intently without interjection.

'I wasn't stupid, you know. I knew from the way she talked and the passions that stirred in her that she was involved in the fight, I knew she hadn't come down to Dublin out of choice. All you had to do back then was turn on the telly and you'd see how bad the troubles were. Car bombs outside of pubs, people being knee-capped for walking down the wrong street, children being spat on and stoned as they walked to school because their parents were the wrong religion. It was a bloody mess and the longer it went on, the more the lines that divided people blurred.'

'But me and your mother, that was separate from us. She knew where I stood as well as I did and we never let it come between us. As much as I disagreed with her beliefs, it was a big part of who she was and because of that, I wouldn't have changed it for anything.'

He pauses for a minute, polishing off the rest of his drink and shifting position in his armchair. I can see by his expression that his thoughts have moved from happier times to something else, something darker.

'But it was different when you boys were born,' he says, anger now brewing beneath the surface. 'It was one thing for your mother growing up in that place but I didn't want any of that for our children. I didn't want her passing on that hatred, that violence to you. You were just kids for God's sake. But you were your mother's son,' he says, leaning forward in his chair and staring at me with those dead eyes. 'You hung on her every word and in the end she poisoned your mind. You know, it broke her heart when you left. It was like the part of her that made her special died, it was there one day and then gone the next.'

There's a tightness in my chest, a pressure that makes it difficult to breathe. The discomfort builds and it takes effort each time I draw a breath.

'I knew,' he says, with a humourless chuckle, 'I knew you'd take up with that shit, it's in your blood. And it was only a matter of time before you went down for it.'

A rasping sound comes up from my throat as I struggle to inhale, but the room is a vacuum and a bead of sweat runs into my eye. My father is smiling now, the smile of the demented. His teeth are yellowed and stained and his breath is a mixture of stale booze and death. He reaches out for me, clawing and pawing his way up my body until my face is cradled in his hands in a parody of affection. I sit motionless and stricken while he grins up at me.

'I know what you did to your brother, Caleb,' he whispers softly to me, 'I know what you did to my boy.'

*It starts like it always does, but this time nothing is the same.
Instead of pulling the car into the driveway, I find myself on foot
walking up toward the front door. The house is different too,
more like I had expected it to be, warm light spilling from every
window and the glow of the porch light guiding me home. The
patter of rain drops on the concrete soothes my itching mind and
I find myself giving into a calm that has been lost to me for so
long it is almost unrecognisable. I jostle for a moment with the
lock before I hear the tumblers slide into place and slowly ease
the door open. A rush of warmth meets me as I enter and on it is
carried the sweet aroma of roast lamb cooking in the oven.
Something catches my eye, a rain jacket belonging to Lily
hanging on the coat rack, red with small cartoon penguins
carrying umbrellas. I smile just for second before a coldness
seeps into my veins and stifles the sentiment that briefly touches
me. Walking down the hall I push on into the kitchen, the blare of
chatter from a small television drones tunelessly alongside the
clicks and hums of appliances. A few toys are littered around the
floor and a stack of newly laundered clothes sits on the counter
top. The dinner table is already set, plates, forks, knives, glasses,
and assorted condiment bottles as a centrepiece. Tacked to the
fridge door are a few photos of happy days, a scrawled grocery
list and a childish drawing of a barnyard scene. Everything
about the room speaks of home, of everyday lives, but nuanced
with the love that fuels those lives. I take a sweater from the top
of the laundry pile and bring it to my face. The fabric is soft and*

fragrant so I close my eyes and draw it in to me. A noise from upstairs shakes me from my thoughts and so I replace the sweater and walk back out into the hallway.

The wood creaks and yawns a little beneath my weight as I climb the staircase but no one calls out. As I round the top stair I can see the movement of shadow and light in the opening of the door before me. Pushing it open, I see Sarah standing by the bed with her back to me, lost in her own thoughts as she folds and sorts laundry. Her hair is tied up in a knot held in place by what looks like two chopsticks. A single errant lock of hair hangs lightly down, drawing my eye to the curvature of her long neck. I have always thought that there is something innocent and untouched about the nape of her neck, something vulnerable yet immutable, the essence of the real Sarah that cannot be disguised of obscured. Something in my bearing makes my presence known and she turns suddenly to face me. 'Caleb,' she says, my name coming in a breathless whisper. She attempts a feeble smile but her eyes betray her, wide pools of fear and weakness. Her breath comes in short catches, her slim shoulders rising and falling with every intake. Her heart pounds so loudly in her chest that I fancy that I can hear it beating. I see her for who she really is and I am filled with hate and loathing. I pull a hunting knife from inside my coat, the weight of the steel and the rubber of the grip feel comfortable in my hand. I slash down at her, her arms instinctively coming up to deflect the arc of the blow. The blade cuts a deep groove into the pale skin of her forearm and she cries out in pain. The knife rises and falls again and again leaving crimson scores criss-crossed on her flesh. I take the blade low and, leaning into it, bury it in her stomach. Her screams are reduced to whimpers as I feel the weight of her body slump forward on the shaft. Pulling out, I hold her up with one hand while I drive the knife home repeatedly, alternating between chest and stomach, stomach and chest. My vision blurs and my muscles begin to ache with the exertion but I continue, allowing the mechanism to take over. The handle of the blade becomes wet and sticky with her blood and I can feel droplets raining down on my skin. Her open wounds bubble and seep, soaking her clothes through. When at last I'm done, I push her body back onto the bed and stare down at her blue eyes, watching them as they glaze over, my body wracked with exhaustion. Wiping the blade on the bed sheets, I secure the knife back inside my coat and leave the room.

Lily is framed in the doorway of her room at the end of the hall. She clutches a ragdoll close to her chest and her face is a picture of worry and terror. She's never seen me before but there is a flicker of something in her eyes, some recognition. At some level she sees her father in me, in the way I move toward her, the way I smile down at her, the way I gather her up in my arms. No sound escapes her as I carry her across the room and lay her down on her bed. Her eyes dart around my face, searching for understanding and the answers to questions she cannot formulate. She lies very still, the ragdoll held tight in her thin arms, and even as I place the pillow down over her face, her expression stills begs for comprehension. It doesn't take long before the thrashing and flailing of her arms and legs is reduced to intermittent spasms and holding the pillow in place causes me no effort at all. When all is still, I leave the pillow covering her face and exit the room.

I walk down the staircase, relaxed now, focused. In the kitchen I move with purpose, turning off appliance after appliance until silence reigns. The kitchen light is turned off, the hallway light, the porch light. I climb the stairs once again and flick the landing switches, plunging the house into a heavy gloom. I re-enter Lily's bedroom and see her on the bed. She's surrounded by her dolls and teddies, lying on her back with her thin arms by her side and the pillow covering her face. This is the way I want it to look, so I leave on a small bedside light. I make my way to the far corner of the room and, opening the closet door, step inside into the shadows. With the door half open I can see the whole room while still being secured in the darkness.

Time becomes meaningless as I stand there listening to the sound of my own breathing. My thoughts are numb, inaccessible, the mechanism has taken over and I allow it to do what it does. At some point the noise of a car engine can be heard approaching, growing louder and slower as it pulls into the driveway. I can see Jacob sitting in the car, I can feel his thoughts in my head. I am an empty shell and Jacob fills me up. His key turns in the lock and he steps into the house, taking off his jacket and hanging it on the coat rack. 'Hello, anybody home?' he calls out but gets no response. I hear him climb the stairs to the landing and call out again, this time softer as if expecting the answer to be close. 'Sarah? Lily?' he asks. A small knock can be heard followed by the creak of a door hinge as he enters her bedroom. I listen to his cries of anguish on finding her, a primal, ancient sound. I feel his horror, I feel his despair, I feel it all. I hear his hands rasp against the wallpaper as he stumbles down the hallway towards the room in which I stand. The door is thrown open and time stands still as the image burns itself into his mind. He falls to the bed and sweeps her limp body up into his arms and, rocking her back and forth, he speaks her name over and over. Lily. Lily. Lily. I reach my arm behind my back, careful not to make a sound and, finding the grip of the pistol, I pull it from my waist band. The metal of the weapon is cold and slick to the touch, its feel formidable. I emerge from my place in the shadows and traverse the distance between us. Something alerts Jacob to my presence and, still cradling Lily in his arms, he turns toward me. From where he now sits on the bed I can see his face soaked with tears, I can see his eyes mad with grief. I can see the flash of recognition as he looks upon me, his only brother in this world. I can see the fear in him as I bring the barrel of the pistol to bear against his forehead. I can see the understanding in his unwavering gaze and the abandon that comes with realisation.

As I pull the trigger I see him die.

I'm pulled from my nightmare by the sounds of festivities coming from the throngs of people in the streets below. From the streaks of muted light that fall through the blinds and stretch long across the floor I can tell that dusk is on us, and the sun is not long for this day. Perspiration sits thick on my chest and stomach and my temples are hot and pricked with fever. I paw absently for a bottle gin on the side table and greedily gulp it down, dribbles escaping down my chin and stinging my flesh. I draw a forearm across my mouth and shake out a cigarette from its packet. My head floats and blue smoke fills the room as the evening light wanes and fades. Finn looks at me from his basket in the corner, his stare cautious and guarded. You're right to be on edge, buddy, I think to myself, I'm not the man you thought I was. I'm not even a man. I'm a monster.

Outside the sounds of Semana Santa echo ominously through the cobbled streets. Holy Week. Black Friday. Already the processions are under way and the funeral band beats out a hypnotic rhythm on the bass drum with cymbal clashes and guttural tuba tones shaking the skies. They celebrate the day that Jesus hung from the cross at Calvary and died for our sins. They weep for the moment when a son cried out to the heavens and gave himself back to his father. When the earth shook and the mountains split and those who would condemn him cowered from the blinding light. No bells are sounded today, no blessed Eucharist received. Today is a day of penance for the sins of man. Today is a day for baptising those who death calls, and anointing those who are sick in spirit. And who among us is more penitent then you, Caleb? Who among us more soul sick and closer to death then you? Who, I ask you, is in more need of deliverance on this day of days?

A mock trial has already been held in the town square at noon and those honoured chosen few replay the hours of His conviction. There stands the Son of God, on trial for masquerading as a false king. There stands Pontius Pilate, beseeching the Jewish leaders to judge Him themselves, but Roman law forbids them from throwing down a sentence of death. There stands Herod of Galilee, whose interrogation of Him finds no guilt. There stands His only Son, bound to a post and lashed until his flesh is torn in shreds and His blood turns the dust to scarlet. And when the punishment is served and the law upheld, Pilate would turn to the people and ask, what would you have me do with this innocent man? And the people would reply, Crucify Him! Crucify Him! In the smaller villages on the outskirts of Antigua, away from prying eyes, the red ribbons of the soldiers whip are replaced with the searing pain of leather and the drops that fall to the soil are pure and true. It is the greatest honour of the chosen man to prostrate himself on the cross in memory of the one true king and offer up his pain in worship when the iron stakes are driven through his palms. Such is the mettle of true conviction, such is the ferocity of unquestionable faith.

There is a pain in my head, an uneven throb that washes in and out like the tides. My guts lurch when the pain peaks and the sensation pulls me from my sick bed and sends me staggering to the bathroom. I fall to my knees and grip the sides of the bowl to steady myself as vomit sprays from my mouth. My body is racked with violence, again and again my guts spasm and scream until the muscles of my stomach cry out in agony. Even when there is nothing left inside me I continue to wretch like the nerve twitch of a corpse long after the life has left it. I can feel my eyes bulge in my skull and consciousness begins to give up the ghost as the air eludes me. Just as the fog pulls me down, I manage to drag in a strangled gasp and I clamber my way back into the world of the living. The cold of the enamel bowl feels good against my forehead, so much so that I forget about the stench of bile and blood that wafts up into my nostrils and slowly clamber to my feet. Turning on the tap in the sink, I splash cold water over my face and hair. I splash it on the back of my neck and on my chest until I feel the fires recede and leave me be. Looking at myself in the mirror I don't recognise anything I see anymore. I look at the ashen pallor of his skin, the sunken shadows of his cheeks. I look at the pale green of his eyes behind which a stranger lies, a stranger who has just awoken from a dream to find himself in a nightmare. A stranger who I thought of as a friend, a trusted confidant, a loved one. I look away in disgust for fear of what I might do if I continue to look upon him, so I throw on a shirt and pants, kiss Finn goodbye and, pulling the door closed behind me, leave this place one last time.

The sun is well set and a black, starless canvas cloaks the earth as I make my way down town. In the distance, Volcán de Fuego splutters and spurts in anger, tearing a molten gash in the night sky. The streets are alive with a manic energy, a fevered pulse that washes through the crowds. Everyone is out tonight, local inhabitants in their droves, generations of families from the surrounding pueblos, tourists from far flung nations, visiting dignitaries, ex-pats, moon-dogs, they're all here tonight. The closer I get to the town square, the thicker the crowd becomes and soon I find myself pushing past bodies and negotiating my way through the masses. My senses feel heightened and open to all that's around me. Clutches of conversations reach my ears as the sea of bodies undulates against me. Fragments of languages I once knew or never heard drift through the air, carried by the sweet voices of young and old, woman and man. A circus of smells assails me, the sticky sweetness of cotton candy from the street vendors, the warm, smoked aroma of grilled chicken from the food stalls, the fresh fragrance of papaya and watermelon that small children hungrily feast on while watching the festivities with wide, enchanted eyes. But behind all of this, the smell of incense creeps forth in a ghostly mist, enveloping everything within its ancient fog.

As I make my way through to the town plaza I catch sight of the main procession still a ways off in the distance. All eyes lean eagerly towards it, the thirst for spectacle and awe demanding to be quenched. Hundreds of men, their purple robes having been changed for the black dress of Good Friday, shoulder the crippling weight of the main float. Atop this burden, surrounded by lavish arrangements of flowers, is a representation of the crucified Christ, his body broken and bleeding beneath a crown of thorns. The men slowly move through the streets as one, their hearts full of penitence but joyous in the fruits their suffering has borne. Behind them, as many women clad in black silken robes bear on their backs the Virgin Mary of Sorrow. Her face has the beatific glow of a loving and grief stricken mother and her hands are joined in prayer for the children of God's earth. The funeral band takes up the rear, their drums sounding out the death knell as they continue on this solemn pilgrimage. All around them, devotees shrouded in black garb keep time, banners and standards proclaiming the wisdom of God's words held high above their heads. Even from this distance I can hear the crowds fall into a still silence as the procession passes close to them, quietened by the inner knowledge that they are baring witness to a manifestation of a love that echoes back centuries into the collective human consciousness. Just for a moment they feel the weight of faith, the toll of belief on the human race and a fundamental connection to one another. If only for a moment.

I cut across the square to escape the crowds and get ahead of the procession's path, breathing shallowly in the stifling mist. As I turn onto Cinta Avenida Norte and walk up towards Kelly's, the crowd thins out to a few stragglers and I take a minute to breathe. Lighting a smoke, I slow to an easy saunter, perhaps grasping at a few moments respite from the overwhelming sense of foreboding that weighs on me like the chains and shackles of an imprisoned man. Approaching the archway, I see a few local women on their knees, hastily making last adjustments to the *alfombras* that cover the street in front of their houses. I stop to admire the intricacy of the work that goes into these carpets. It is, as it has always been, tradition to lay a decorative bed on the cobbled streets to facilitate the float bearers during the Black Friday processions. A bed of sand is first spread on the stones to create an even surface. Dyed sawdust in vibrant, reds, yellows, whites and purples are added to the carpet using stencils of intricate and boundless design. These creations are painstakingly

116

applied and are the accumulation of months of labour and planning by each family. Finally, seeds and plants, flowers and vegetables are used to decorate and enhance the art work until its completion. The *alfombra* encapsulates the essence of Mayan culture and tradition while embracing biblical symbolism and the ever present importance of the natural world. Hearing the sounds of the procession slowly approaching in the far off distance, I think of how this creation will be inevitably destroyed underfoot and, for a moment, I'm touched by a pang of sadness. But maybe that's the point of it all, maybe it's a testament to man's folly in the pursuit of permanence. Maybe it shows how diligence and the labour of love are always worthy even when you know the end is near. It is, after all, the nature of all things to rage against the dying of the light, but that inevitable end does not negate a life of truth and meaning. If anything it should make the fires burn all the brighter for it.

Lost in distraction, I notice one of the women looking up at me as if she has been doing so for some time. She's younger than the other women, perhaps not even in her twenties, and her brown cheeks are flushed with the work. Her eyes are bright and clear and, as she looks up at me and smiles, I feel embarrassed by her gaze. I feel ashamed for the way I look, I feel ashamed for what I am. I'm reminded of the beast that lives in my soul and the poison that runs in my veins. I turn my face from her in anger and self-loathing but I feel her hand touch mine and I look down to see her beckon me to my knees. Without words she gestures to the clay bowls of coloured sawdust and motions for me to help her fill in the last of the surface. I work on an image of the Sacred Heart framed in an aura of golden light with a fiery cross at its head. As I toil, I find myself floating on a sea of catharsis, allowing it to cool my fevered brow, but as I smooth down the last of the red sawdust into the edges of the heart I see that my hands have become stained with dye. Using my own spittle I try to rub it off but, try as I may, the pigment remains, ingrained deep into the grooves and cracks of my skin.

The bells of La Merced are silent as I step in through the doors of Kelly's. The place is more or less deserted, save for one or two old timers nodding off in the corner. I assume most of the regulars have dragged themselves off stool and wandered down town to take in the atmosphere of the night, which suits me just fine. I can't pretend to be in control of myself and as such feel capable of anything. This is a house of answers and I won't be walking away until I'm sated.

Lucas stands alone by the bar nursing a tumbler of whisky and motions to Pedro to rack up a couple more when he sees me arrive. He's dressed as per usual in a fine black shirt open at the collar with the sleeves rolled back to reveal his tanned, sinewy forearms. There's something uneasy in his stance and, as I approach, he takes off his black-rimmed glasses and begins to vigorously polish the pink lenses with the edge of his shirt. He's quiet as I come up beside him, giving me a small smile in lieu of his usual gregarious welcome. We both look on silently as Pedro fills our glasses and, glancing first to me and then to Lucas, he leaves the bottle with us and walks away down the far end of the bar. Drinking deeply from my whisky, I savour the moment, feeling the slow burn as my thirst is quenched, feeling that shiver of pleasure as my whole being responds to its lover's touch. Lucas crushes the last of his cigarillo in an ashtray and turns to give me his full attention. There is a seriousness about him that I haven't seen before. That somewhat boyish smirk that never strays far from his mouth is nowhere to be seen and for the first time he looks old to me. His eyes are full of the warmth and compassion that comes with our friendship but they are also filled with a weary sadness.

'Hello, Caleb,' he says simply, the name sounding comfortable and familiar on his tongue as if he's being speaking it all his life. I stand and stare at Lucas for an unknown length of time, stunned by the feeling that I've been falling forever only to suddenly hit the ground. The wind has been knocked out of me, my body crushed, my spirit smashed to pieces. When I finally find words and regain the ability to use them, I lean in close to Lucas and speak.

'How could you not tell me?' I whisper, imploring him with a voice that trembles with seething rage and incomprehension. 'You've known all this time, haven't you? I can see it in your fucking face, you've known all this time, while I've been sat here pouring out my fucking heart day after day, you've known all along and didn't tell me. I thought you were my fucking friend, Lucas!' I have a fistful of his shirt in my grip but there's no power in my limbs and, as my legs give way from under me, he takes my weight in his arms and helps me onto a bar stool.

'I'm sorry, Caleb, I'm sorry,' he says, steadying me where I sit before stepping back. 'I am your friend and you're mine, and in all the time I've known you I've never lied to you, but I couldn't tell you. As much as it pained me not to, it simply wasn't my place to say. You had to work it out yourself, Caleb, that's the only way it can happen. Things are the way they are, and as much as I would have liked to intervene, I'm still a part of it, and I must adhere to the natural order of things.'

I watch him as his mouth moves and I listen to the words as they leave him. I recognise the order in which they're placed but the sequence holds no meaning for me. I know what it is he's saying but I can't apply significance to the whole. My reality cracks and splinters as I try to connect what he's saying to something I know to be true, but my entire frame of reference has been revealed to be a lie. I thought I knew who I was but I was wrong, and so those truths lie in shattered shards around my feet, figments of a broken mind.

'But I remember,' I say quietly, groping desperately at those fragments, 'I remember everything I've gone through to find Caleb.' Even saying the name sends chords of panic and nausea through me and I grip the edge of the bar like it was the last sliver of driftwood on the open seas.

'Do you, Caleb?' asks Lucas, softly, placing a hand on my shoulder. 'What is it you remember? What is it you remember of your life before the day you walked in through these doors and pulled up a seat at the bar. Think, Caleb! Think back to the very moment you decided to pursue this path.'

I see myself standing by Sarah and Lily's grave, their coffins have already been smothered with earth. I'd never seen a coffin that size before, its diminutive proportions adding another layer of surreal horror to the occasion. I see myself standing there, black suit, black tie, black shoes, black. The rest of the mourners who came to pay their last respects have long gone, leaving me to my grief. As I stand by the graveside my sorrow begins to take form, begins to mutate into something my tortured mind can grasp. My grief reshapes itself into purpose, adapting and evolving to protect its host from extinction. In that moment my resolve becomes meaning and my objective becomes the very thing I am. I see myself systematically deconstructing my life, pushing away all those who ever cared about me. I remember thinking how easy that was, how you somehow expect people to hold onto you for dear life, refusing to be cast aside. But the reality of things is different. Relationships are built on reciprocated feelings and self-validation mirrored by your peers. Once you alter that dynamic, once you become an outsider, there is a part of people that wishes you to disappear lest you threaten the delicate balance that is their constructed reality.

I see myself as a man reborn, a new creature not yet defined. I see myself living on the road, sleeping in shitty hotels, travelling cross country by bus, spending as little as possible to ensure I can go the distance. It was the logical assumption that Caleb would be in the wind, knowing that I would never let it stand, that I would never be at peace as long as he walked the earth. He was, after all, my brother, and we knew each other at an intimate level. I knew that if I was to find him, I would have to think like him, act like him, become him. And that's exactly what I did. I closed my eyes and let myself be guided by Caleb. I was the needle of a compass and, left to spin freely, I would find sure north. Every choice I made, every route I took, the things I ate, the way I dressed, the cut of my hair and beard. I took odd jobs to replenish my funds, jobs that Caleb would have chosen. I worked a stretch as a utility man on a battered old oil tanker called the Nightingale. The tasks were menial and in some cases demoralising, mopping the decks, doing the crew's laundry, helping out with galley duties, but the pay was good when you were on the ocean for so long and the sea air made me feel robust, invigorated. When we stopped to refuel off the east coast of Nicaragua I felt Caleb's scent was strong and I struck out across land, certain in the feeling I was closing on him. Weeks turned into months as I slowly made my way north. I was unrelenting in my method, sacrificing time, comfort and to some extent sanity to make sure I lived as Caleb, every choice, no matter how insignificant, being my brothers.

Just as I began to give up hope and stray from my course, I met a man working in the central bus terminal in Tegucigalpa who recognised Caleb from a crumpled photo I carried on me. It was the break I'd been waiting for, and I felt that all my hard work had not been in vain. My resolve was strengthened and I set off with new zeal, fresh eyed and hungry. It wasn't until I talked to a coffee farmer in the small town of San Pedro on the shores of Lake Atitlan that I caught another break. The old man said that Caleb had worked for a spell labouring on his land and, on leaving, had told the man that he was heading for Antigua. It was with that knowledge in hand that I first stepped in through these doors in search of my brother.

As I remember these things, as I weigh the cost of my commitment, I feel Lucas' eyes on me. His unflinching gaze burrows deep inside, watching these memories trace their way across my mind. I feel the clarity of these images begin to fade, the sharpness of their colour, the edges of their detail begin to flake and peel. I clamber to grip hold of these past moments as they one by one crumble to dust. Crisp colour becomes pastel shades and then the jaded grey of ghosts. I see past the memories to the truth beneath, I see that they are nothing but figments of my sick imagination. Pages from books, forgotten scenes from movies, half-remembered stories, snatches from the lives of others. All these things, pasted together in a grim collage, held in place by the memory whisper of old emotions and the hidden desires of a life unlived.

Sitting on the barstool, feeling the uneven grain of the wooden counter beneath my hands, memories once lost to me begin to bubble to the surface. We're boys of ten or eleven years old and we're lying on our beds listening to a heated exchange between our parents below. Something I did in school is the reason that the argument began and I lie with my face buried in my pillow and cry. I remember the feeling of the damp fabric against my face, warm and wet from my tears. Something has changed in this moment, something in the way we perceive our parents has been irrevocably altered and the experience causes us pain and distress. After the fight has slowly bled out of them we hear their footfalls on the stairs and they come into our room to talk with us. My mother takes my head in her lap and sits quietly stroking away the tears from my flushed cheeks while my father explains how rumours we had heard that day were just lies concocted by small minds. But I know the true liar has revealed himself. I listen to him as he denies my mother's heart, betrayal and cowardice twisting his words. I see him now for what he is and I begin to hate him.

I'm a young man of eighteen or nineteen and I'm roused from a groggy half-sleep by the sound of Sarah quietly gathering up her clothes from where they fell to the floor the night before. My head aches from the drink and I squint up at her in the grey morning light. She's dressed only in her underwear and has on the tee-shirt I was wearing last night. It's a few sizes too big for her and it makes her look somehow childish. With her make-up slightly smeared and her hair tangled, it occurs to me that I've never seen anything so beautiful before in all my life. She notices me looking up at her and her expression becomes peculiar, conflicted. I can't read her at all but I experience an unsettling feeling in the pit of my stomach. She leans down over the bed and kisses me hard on the lips, her mouth half-open, moist and sweet. When she pulls away it's as if all of the emotion has drained from her and she's as cold as stone. Fixing me with a penetrating look she says, 'that's the last time I'll ever kiss you.' And then she leaves me.

I'm a grown man, standing in the shade of a willow tree in a small city park. Across a green pond, beneath the boughs of a gnarled horse-chestnut tree sits a couple in love. They have spread out an old blanket on the grass and Jacob sits with his back against the trunk, while Sarah lays her head in his lap and gazes up at the clear blue skies. He reads to her from a small paperback and she wears a dreamy smile as she gets lost in the world her paints for her. He looks down at her and, cupping her cheek in his hand, he says something to her that makes her laugh. Standing there alone in the half shadow, her laughter burns me like drops of molten lead on my heart.

I'm drunk, sitting at the far corner of a hotel bar, watching the distorted images from my past refracted through a wall of split mirrors behind the counter. I see old friends and distant cousins dancing and making merry. I see my mother sitting quietly, sipping on a white wine soda with a distant smile on her face, nodding to well-wishers as they come and go. I see my father deep in conversation with a group of faceless men, a high colour on his cheeks from the drink, his hands gesturing wildly and a squint in his eye. I see Sarah, dazzling and flawless in a simple white dress, negotiating the room with charm and ease. And all of it belongs to Jacob. There he stands, preening in his new suit, laughing and joking with everyone, exchanging furtive, knowing glances with his new bride. My thoughts are blurred and poisonous and the booze sits heavy on me. I watch Jacob through the mirror until my eyes begin to scald, I watch him as he enjoys what should have been mine. I watch him as he lives my life.

I'm a prisoner, slumped in my cot, the din of the other inmates fading in the distance as the drugs take effect. I don't count the months or the weeks or the days or the minutes. Freedom is just one more thing to be taken from me. It's not enough to strip a man of everything he loves and leave him exiled in misery. It's not enough that he be forced to press up against the glass of the real world and watch as the lives of others unfold. No, he must also be caged like an animal. He must also be shackled at the wrists and ankles, made fight for the slops, be watched while he shits. Strip me of everything and all you will do is find the monster that lives at the core. And when you do, thief, when you tear away at my flesh and release the beast that sleeps, my vengeance will rain down on you in white fire and you will look me in the eye and know that it is me who has taken everything from you.

Lucas and I sit in silence, with only the distant sound of the approaching procession still a ways off. The dull thump of the base drum and the mournful song of the tuba come in a ghostly echo through Antigua's streets. As I look out the door I see the mist of incense has begun to creep down towards us, beginning to smother the street lights in its cotton embrace. I down my whisky and run my tongue over my lips before lighting a smoke and breathing a heavy sigh. I turn to Lucas and see that his eyes have never left me this whole time.

'But why here, Lucas?' I ask, softly, 'why have I come all the way here. What is this place?'

'This is a place of answers, Caleb. Most of the time the answers are easy but it's the questions that cause us the most pain.'

'I don't understand,' I say, looking at Lucas in bewilderment.

'I know,' he answers, in a soothing tone, 'it's a difficult and painful journey but one that everyone must eventually take. I know how hard it's been for you, Caleb, but as I said before, I've always been your friend.' He takes the bottle of scotch from the counter and fills both our glasses before he speaks again. And when he does, his voice is even and serious.

'You never finished your story, Caleb,' he says. I cough out a bitter laugh and favour him with an incredulous look.

'You seem to know more about me than I do, my friend,' I say, shaking my head and taking a gulp from my glass, but Lucas remains insistent.

'Everyone's got to tell their own story, and you still have a bit left in yours,' he says, patiently.

Well, if it's a confession you want from me, my one true friend, it's a confession you'll get.

'My name is Caleb,' I say, anger beginning to seep into my voice, anger at myself, anger at Lucas. 'I went to my brother's house, his home, when I knew he wouldn't be there. I went there when I knew it would only be his wife and daughter all alone. I broke into his home to steal from him, to rob from him all the things that matter most in his life.' My voice begins to catch in my throat and hot tears well up in my eyes. 'I took the woman he loved and I cut her. I drove my knife into her until there was nothing left, just a broken body. I took his daughter, little Lily,' I say, the tremble in my hands spreading throughout my body, 'I took her, and I held a pillow over her face until she stopped breathing and then I left her lying there so it was the first thing her father saw when he entered the room. I hid and waited for Jacob to come home from work. I listened to his pain when he found Sarah, I watched from the shadows as he cradled the body of his little girl. I watched as the soul was wrenched from his body and I smiled as his grief broke him in two.' The tears are rolling down my cheek and my voice is barely intelligible through the tremors. 'I put a gun to his head and looked him right in the eye as I pulled the trigger. I murdered my only brother.' I sit there, deflated and empty, not able to look Lucas in the eye.

'Finish the story, Caleb,' says Lucas, taking me firmly by the arm.

'What the fuck are you talking about?' I cry through the tears, 'Is that not enough for you? What more do you want from me? I've told you everything, haven't I?'

'Remember, Caleb, remember!' he says, his face warped through the curtain of tears. His hand tightens its grip on me and I feel a sharp pain emanating through my muscles. My body shudders with spasms as the tremors hammer down a ceaseless assault. It's too much for me. I can feel myself slipping down into the fog, I can hear Lucas calling my name from a distance, and then I become enveloped by the darkness.

I'm standing in the closet with nothing but the sound of my own breathing. At some point the noise of a car engine can be heard approaching, growing louder and slower as it pulls into the driveway. My thoughts reach out to my brother like tentacles slithering through the gloom in search of sustenance. I imagine myself stepping inside him, feeling what he feels, becoming him. I want to know every emotion that runs in him and my senses tingle with anticipation. I want him to know pain and loss, I want him to know what true emptiness feels like. My nerve endings bristle like open receptors and, my veins, conduits to his misery. I hear his cries on finding his beloved Sarah and it fills me up. I see him burst through the door and gather up Lily in his arms and I smile to myself. I smile in the darkness. I emerge from the closet with gun in hand and move across the room to where a father sits, rocking his daughter back and forth. Something alerts him to my presence at his back and he turns to see me standing before him. I can taste his fear as he confronts his nightmare and I watch recognition bleed into his face and eyes as he sees me for who I am. But there is nothing left in him. The person he thought he was is now gone and he welcomes the gift I bring him. I place the barrel of the pistol against his forehead and, as he looks up at me, I let the hammer fall. I stand for a moment staring down at my brother, my arms limp by my side. I feel nothing but the beating of my own heart in my chest. Raising the gun one last time, I place the barrel in my mouth and feeling the metal hot against my skin, I squeeze the trigger once more.

I gasp for breath, my eyes wide and bulging and my face dripping wet. Lucas is standing over me with an empty glass, concern etched on his features. I'm lying on the floor and the light behind Lucas' head creates a shimmering halo around him. He smiles down at me and I notice something I never noticed before. He is beautiful. He offers me his hand and I take it, allowing him to pull me to my feet. Everything is different now, the texture of surfaces more vivid, the lines sharper. It feels as if

I've lived a life out of focus and for the first time I see it all with crystal clarity. I have emerged from a dream to find my life is no more real then the imagined world I had created for myself. But now I have that which eluded me for so long, the dawn of understanding.

I take a seat at the bar and pour another two fingers into each glass. Lucas pulls up his seat beside me and we raise a toast to the night. Turning to him, I ask one thing of my old friend, 'Tell me a story, Lucas. Tell me your story.' He sits quiet for a minute, then begins to speak, his eyes lost in memories of the past.

'Once upon a time, I thought I knew the nature of things, I thought I understood. I believed we were all free beings in the universe and I too marvelled at its beauty and perfection. I was a loyal and true soldier who, like many others, simply accepted the role that was thrust upon him, happy to know he served a kingdom greater than himself. But a kingdom is only as great as its king. I moved through the ranks with ease until I commanded many legions, soldiers who knew me and loved me. The king's eyes fell on me and he loved me too, as I loved him, and I sat at his right hand and, in many things, had the king's ear. But from where I sat, I began to see the king for what he truly was, flawed. The crown sits heavy on all, and if worn too long, there are none that can escape its crushing weight. The king isolated himself from his subjects and toiled in secrecy for the longest time. He distanced himself from those who loved him and, in his absence, I spoke for him and all before me listened. When the king returned, he brought with him a man, a simple man of no substance. He gathered his kingdom around him and presented this simple man for all to see. When they had looked upon him, the king commanded all his followers to bow down before this man, this man of no substance. But I refused. Who was this creature that stood before me? Who was he to deserve my knee?

The king was enraged, maddened by my disobedience. He accused me of hubris and called me usurper. So incensed was he, that he banished me from his kingdom along with my closest allies. We were cast out, and the gates of the kingdom were forever shut behind us. Like all kingdoms, loyalty breeds in the face of a common enemy and I became known as the adversary.'

Although Lucas' eyes are half closed, searching out the memories from where they sleep, I can tell by him that this process causes him hurt. He now exists between time, both reliving the past and experiencing it afresh in this moment. My heart goes out to him as his sits quietly, sipping on his whisky, trying to articulate his thoughts. Turning to me now, he draws from new energy and continues purposefully with clear eyes.

'The universe seeks balance, even down to the energy of the smallest particle, and thus all things are defined by this,' he says, punctuating his speech with hand gestures. 'There is no good without evil. There is no spring without winter. What is darkness if there is no light? The entire perception of reality is polarised and therefore we seek out the balance to define what we are. In truth, I am no more the adversary than you are, Caleb. I simply serve the balance which makes me nothing more than his servant, even in exile.'

'I have been called many things in the past and by some I was known as the one who bears the light. From the beginning, when I looked upon that simple man, I saw him for what he was. I tried to speak out against this affront to the balance of things, to show that there was too much darkness in his being and that it would lead to disease, a sickness that would eat away at the very fabric of the void. But his vanity was so, that he was blinded by the beauty of his own creation and could not see it for what it truly was. On casting me out, he removed question, liability. He became infallible.'

'Although I served the balance, I still endeavoured to show the truth of man, to shine the light on his true self for all to see.

From the first time in the garden when I whispered in the woman's ear, all I have ever wanted is to illuminate the rotten core of his existence. But I have been damned for my honesty. You see, Caleb, I'm tired. I'm tired of looking upon his creation and seeing the scourge that is humanity. You now understand more than anyone the true nature of things, what man really is deep inside and the pain and misery he causes. Of course, men of faith try to control the people and their holy houses aren't yet empty, but this is just another system of control, a lie. Their weapons of persuasion have changed over the centuries, cold steel and the lick of flame replaced by the subtle flicker of a forked tongue as the seeds of guilt are planted in the hearts of those who would seek the truth. Lies begetting lies. And there is no place for lies in the balance. And what is faith anyway, but blindness? All it does is make slaves of men.'

The fog of incense has begun to thicken in the street, and its wisps and curls begin to creep inside to where we sit. The procession is nearly upon us, the drums growing louder as the minutes pass. It won't be long now before an army of the devout is at the door. I drink down my whisky and I drink down his words, tasting them, feeling them.

'True humanity, I mean the one we keep so thinly veiled, is inherently monstrous. Think for a moment of how the true evil doers of history are talked about. Sure, there is the morally appropriate disgust implicit in the retelling of the tales, but the stories themselves are spoken of in hushed voices, awe filled, almost giddy with the brief glimpse of what they know to be real humanity, what lies behind the mask. As if the telling and retelling of these acts nourish their secret souls. History's saints are reluctantly acknowledged also, but with barely concealed boredom, revealed through bland and lifeless words. The rhetoric of war is full of passion and fire while the language of peace is grey and stillborn. Fundamentally, man knows what he is, beyond the shackles of institutional slavery.'

'And when man looks on violence and death and feels his cock stiffen, it's not some primal instinct to propagate the species in response to the sight of ones own mortality. No, it's the visceral ecstasy at seeing the truth, humanities true face in the mirror. Despite facades, we tear this world to ruin. The streets and rivers run red with the legacy of man, tearing and clawing at the gifts of life. He has become fluent in the language of denial and self deception, conjuring abstractions to cloak the reality of his thirst. Misdirection and illusion employed to remove accountability. I have been called a pusher of earthly sin, but the reality is that man was born an addict. From the time he drinks from his mother's breast to when he is hunched and grey with dust for bones, man craves it with all of his being. They inherit the world and they watch it burn. And that, my friend, is the true nature of the beast.'

Through the mist I see the procession pass outside, not long now until His final resting place is reached. I squint through teary eyes, the acrid fog tasting like ash in my mouth. I can make out the black robed silhouettes wearily bearing His weight home. The crash of the symbols and the bellow of the tuba are deafening now, coming from all around. I fill my glass and, looking out to the streets, I raise a toast to them. My ears are filled with an unsettling laughter that I can't hold in, nor would I want to.

'Do you understand what I'm trying to tell you, Caleb? I'm not judging or damning man for what he has done, I'm simply showing him for what he truly is, a mistake. And this is why I have chosen you, my friend, why I chose to be your companion on this journey. I have been by your side in it all, never coercing or condemning, just offering you support through these hard times. And now, when you have walked through fire and come out the other side, I'm still standing here, as your friend. Because of these trials, because of your awakening, you, Caleb, have the capacity to understand the futility of it all. You were lost and now you are found. You have witnessed the cost of it, experienced the pain of it and now comprehend how meaningless it all is. I am showing you the truth because what makes you special to him makes you special to me. You see, you're different, Caleb. There have only ever been a few who can bear the weight of the gift he gave you and not have their sanity torn from them. And it's that gift that I would ask you to use one more time, my friend. You see everything now for what it is. You have experienced first hand the true nature of mankind and all I have done is opened your eyes. I too am locked into this grim waltz of existence and after an eternity of struggle I have nothing left to give. It falls to you to right the wrong, Caleb. You are Dante, you are djinn, you are free will.'

Lucas gets to his feet and stands beside me, so close that the hairs on my neck respond to the softness of his breath. I struggle to lift my head to meet his eyes, the burden of drink taking its toll on this broken man. The sweet aroma of honey and a floral scent I can't quite recognise fills my nose and lungs. Lucas removes his glasses and places them on the bar counter and I see him for the first time. His eyes are the lightest blue I have ever seen and there is a kinetic quality to them, like the slow tumble of smoke through water. He reaches out his hand and gently brushes a tear from my cheek. I expect his touch to be coarse and rough but it feels silken against my fevered flesh. He plants a soft kiss on my temple, a simple act, timeless. It was the last he had to give and now he is empty.

Pedro has emerged behind the bar and saunters down to our end. I've seen him a hundred times but only the once like this. He pays Lucas no heed and stops before me, the bar creaking a little as he leans his massive bulk to address me close. I can see him taking the measure of me with his cold eyes, assessing the sum of me. Action or speech seem futile to me so I stare blankly and wait. There's something there, a slight twitch in the muscle of his eyebrow that betrays a hesitancy in him, but the moment passes and he speaks the words I knew would come.

'It's time for you to go, Caleb,' he says. As simple as that. It's time for me to go. I drain my glass, bang it down on the counter, and smack my lips with relish.

'It appears it is, buddy,' I say, a wide smile spreading across my face. I pat down the pockets of my shirt and trousers and affect a look of chagrin. 'Jeez, it seems like I forgot my wallet. Is it okay if I hit you next time round?' The shadow of a sneer curls his lip and he simply sends me on my way with a nod towards the door at the far end of the room. I slide off the barstool and slowly walk across the floor, never once looking back. I rap on the door lightly and then slip inside, pulling it shut behind me.

Uri is sitting at his desk bent over some ancient tome, scrutinizing detail through an oval magnifying glass. He looks up as I enter and smiles his wolfish smile, the meat of his gums pink and shiny.

'Ah yes, Caleb,' he says, matter of factly, waving me in and gesturing to the seat across from him, 'Please, please.' Taking a seat I peer at the large book before him. The language is unknown to me, the symbols more foreign than anything I've ever know, and its pages are coated in a fine layer of pink dust. Uri seems positively merry as he closes it over with a heavy clap and places it on the floor beside him.

'You've done well, Caleb, better than anyone could have expected,' he says to me, as if he were giving a treat to some fucking mutt who just learned how to fetch. Look at this smug cunt, sitting there leering at me in his white fucking suit, with his white fucking shoes. But I keep my mask on straight, I show nothing. I have become skilled at the art of imitation, an emotional chameleon, a one time prisoner of my own art but now I am free and the mask is mine to wear. I enjoy how it feels on me and I smile through it. I sit and listen as he rambles on, this repugnant thing, I sit and peer at him through the eye holes and I am disgusted by him. I remember the fear I felt as I sat in this chair as another man, as I sat and trembled before the things unknown, and I am disgusted by him too. Disgusted by his weakness, disgusted by his pathetic life.

As I watch him drone on, I feel a strange sensation come over me, as if my head has opened up and I can perceive everything at once. As if all existence, past and present, has been reduced to a single point. I see the blackness of space and the infinite array of stars, the patterns of the cosmos splashed across the great canvas. I see the hidden depths of the earth's oceans and the white peaks of its mountains, the sands of its deserts lain out before me and the frozen heart of its forgotten plains. I see the creatures of the sea, beasts of the earth and birds of the sky, and I know them all by name and know their soul. I see the dawn of civilisations, the complex evolution of cultures, the perseverance of tradition, the monuments to forever. I see birth and death, life and love, tears and destruction. I look closer and I see the dust that makes up everything and, for a fraction of time, I understand it all. And then I see me, Caleb, a man of men.

As Uri leans back in his chair, his fingers tented on his belly, his wasted words are interrupted by a soft chiming sound. We both look to the old brass clock that sits on his desk. Its single hand is pointed directly at twelve and a minute hammer strikes the small silver bell housed within its casing. The sound is beautiful and full for such a small device and it fills the room, its harmonics resonating from every corner. When its song has run down, the cogwheels behind the copper mesh cease their labour and the clock ticks no more.

'Well, it's time, Caleb,' he says, eyeing me from across the table. He doesn't get to his feet, but instead looks toward the heavy wood door at the other side of the room and gestures to it with his hand. 'Goodbye,' he says.

My legs quiver a little as I walk but I steady myself and climb the two steps that lead up to the door. Dust particles play in the light that steals its way under its solid wooden heft and, as I approach it, I tentatively place my fingertips against its grainy surface. I fancy I can feel a pulse beating within its dark red crevices or it may just be the swollen throb of my own heart. I place my hand on the ornate, wrought iron handle and push the door open, the creak of its ancient hinges crying out as the light washes over me. I bathe in it, imagining it to be a light without colour, brighter than any light before yet it doesn't hurt my eyes to look on it. As I step across the threshold and feel the light envelop me, my lips move to form a word I never knew, but have uttered many times before. As I'm swallowed up and the door begins to close behind me, I speak this word one final time.

And then there was nothing.

THE END

Breinigsville, PA USA
14 April 2011
259866BV00001B/30/P

9 781908 200150